"White, no. Pink, yes," Casey announced.

"What did you say?" Jake asked.

"White, no. Pink, yes."

Casey's eyes were fixed on the plastic stick in front of her as if it meant life or death. Irritation simmered inside him. He glanced around the room, looking for clues. Suddenly his gaze landed on an unfolded set of instructions lying half in the sink. Frowning, he reached for them at the same moment she spoke again.

"Since it's pink, do you suppose that means it's a girl? No," she continued, "pink just means pregnant. It could be a boy."

Girl? Boy? Jake's mouth went dry and his brain blanked out. Was she saying what he thought she was saying? No. Of course not.

But when she lifted her head and met his gaze through wide teary eyes, he knew it was true.

"Congratulations, Jake. We're pregnant...."

MAUREEN CHILD

The Surprise Christmas Bride

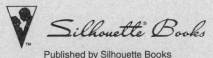

Silhouette Books

Published by Silhouette Books

America's Publisher of Contemporary Romance

ISBN-13: 978-0-373-19896-2
ISBN-10:   0-373-19896-5

THE SURPRISE CHRISTMAS BRIDE

MAUREEN CHILD

Maureen Child is a California native who loves to travel. Every chance they get, she and her husband are taking off on another research trip. The author of more than sixty books, Maureen loves a happy ending and still swears that she has the best job in the world. She lives in Southern California with her husband, two children and a golden retriever with delusions of grandeur.

You can contact Maureen via her Web site: www.maureenchild.com.

To the gang at Sunshine Books:
Nita, Betty and Ron.
You guys are the best.

One

"Maybe I should put the top up before I drown."

Casey Oakes pushed wet hair out of her eyes and squinted into the freezing rain. A deep hard shiver rippled through her. "Too late now to bother," she grumbled, and told herself that maybe it would be a blessing if she *did* drown. At least then she would have done something no other Oakes had ever managed. Drowning in a convertible while cruising the back roads outside Simpson, California, wasn't, as her mother would say, "what society expects of an Oakes."

Accomplishing that feat in a wedding gown would only add to the myth, she told herself. A few years from now, her little ride would probably become the stuff of local folklore. People would tell the story of Cassandra Oakes in hushed tones around campfires. Parents would discipline misbehaving children with the threat of a nighttime visit from the Drowned Bride.

Still smiling to herself, Casey flinched when her soggy veil flew in front of her face and blocked her view of the road. She slammed on the brakes, heard something under her car snap, then came to a shuddering halt.

She cut the engine, and when that powerful noise disappeared, all that was left was the sound of the heavy rain pelting on and all around her. The windshield wipers continued to slap rhythmically as they futilely tried to do battle with the downpour. Nearly an inch of water covered the floorboards, no doubt ruining the plush scarlet carpet. Casey winced as she realized that the leather seats probably weren't faring any better.

"Well, hell," she muttered to no one, "who expected rain?" But then, with the way the rest of her day had gone, why *not* rain? Heck, why not a blizzard?

Reaching up, she pushed her veil to the back of her head and looked around at the drenched countryside. The road wasn't much more than a narrow dirt track, covered yearly by a thin layer of gravel. Now the ground-up rock was practically floating atop a sea of churning mud. On either side of the road wooden fence posts, strung with barbed wire, stood at attention for miles. Behind those fences lay open ground. Meadow grasses, waving and dipping with the wind and rain, a few gnarled leafless trees that looked as though they'd been there for centuries, a veritable forest of giant pines, their needles dipping with the weight of the rain—and that was it.

No houses.

No lights.

No people.

To top it all off, it had been so long since she'd been back in Simpson she didn't know if she was close to the Parrish ranch or not.

Casey inhaled sharply and felt the familiar sting of tears filling her eyes. Roughly she brushed them away with the backs of her hands.

She already had all the water she could handle.

Then she heard it.

The call came softly at first, then built into a low throbbing moan.

Frowning, Casey stepped out of the car and grimaced as the cold mud oozed over the tops of her white satin pumps. When her right foot slid out from under her in the muck, she forgot all about her ruined shoes. She grabbed at the car door for balance and managed somehow to keep from landing facedown in the thick brown river at her feet.

"Yuck." A sucking noise accompanied the movement as she lifted one shoeless foot from the icy mud. She heard the moaning sound again and turned her head to find the source.

Her eyes widened and a rush of sympathy for something besides herself washed over her.

"Oh, you poor little thing," she crooned, and started slogging through the mud.

"No, I don't want to tell you what it is." Jake Parrish laughed, shook his head and reached for his coffee cup. His sister, Annie, hadn't changed a bit over the years. Grown-up or not, she still couldn't stand suspense.

"C'mon Jake," she pleaded over the phone. "One little hint. Just one."

"Nope," he told her, and took a sip of coffee. "You'll just have to get out here first thing in the morning if you want your curiosity satisfied."

"You really are an evil man, big brother."

"Yeah, I know." He grinned, then added, "Oh, and would you mind bringing Dad, Uncle Harry and Aunt Emma, too?"

Annie sucked in a gulp of air and Jake could almost

see his younger sister's black eyebrows shooting into her hairline. Lord, how she hated not knowing everything.

"This must be big," she finally said.

"Big enough," Jake assured her.

"Dammit, Jake!" Annie's voice dropped into the stern no-nonsense tone she used on her three-year-old, Lisa. "You know I hate surprises. If you don't give me something to go on, I won't get a wink of sleep all night."

She wouldn't, either. Memories rushed through him. The night before her birthday, Annie would lie awake all night, wondering what she might receive. And Christmas Eve was even worse. Then she was so bad not only did *she* stay awake, she kept Jake up, too.

"All right," he said with a smile. "One little hint."

"Yesss!"

Jake frowned thoughtfully as he tried to figure out a way to phrase the hint without giving away too much of his surprise. He leaned back against the kitchen wall, crossed his feet at the ankles and stared up at the overhead light fixture. Shaped like a wagon wheel, the chandelier held six globe-covered lightbulbs, which shone brightly against the late-afternoon gloom.

He shifted his gaze to the storm raging outside the window. Thanks to the deal he'd just managed to pull off, he told himself, not even the torrential rain or predicted snow could ruin his good mood.

"Jake..."

"Oh! Sorry, Annie. Just thinkin'."

"Don't strain yourself."

"Very funny. Maybe I won't give you that hint, after all."

"Jake Parrish, if you don't..."

He laughed and pushed away from the wall. "OK, you win. Here's your hint. It's something I've wanted for a long time."

A lengthy silent pause. Then, "that's *it?*" Outrage colored her voice.

"That's it. Until tomorrow."

"I said it before and I'll say it again. You're an evil man, Jake. And you're going to hell."

"Probably. But that's all right. At least all of my friends will be there with me."

"Count on it."

In answer he gave her a deep-throated malevolent chuckle. He wasn't surprised to hear her hang up in disgust.

Oh, he knew his little sister would find a way to make him pay for dragging this out. But dammit, it would be worth it. He'd waited a long time for this. And he wanted to enjoy every minute of it.

He hung up the phone, walked across the room to the gray granite countertop and set his coffee cup down. Then he leaned forward to peer through the rain-spattered glass at the growing darkness. This was just the beginning, he told himself.

With the conclusion of this deal, his long-held plans for the Parrish ranch were complete at last. Now he could focus on the horse-breeding program he'd been thinking about for months.

Anything was possible.

A slow grin tipped up one corner of his mouth as he took a quick look around the kitchen. Modern appliances, a gleaming Spanish-tile floor and a kiva-shaped fireplace in the corner made the kitchen something of a showplace. Not that he could do anything more complicated than a pot of coffee, grilled cheese sandwiches and an assortment of microwavable delights.

That didn't matter, though. For Jake had made good on his promises. He had turned the ranch into a business prosperous enough to pay off all the cosmetic changes to the house that his ex-wife had insisted on. And despite Linda's efforts, she hadn't managed to empty his pockets.

Jake frowned slightly at the memory of the woman he had allowed to make a fool of him, but then he dismissed all thoughts of her. Instead, he concentrated on the ranch. His accomplishment. His triumph. The place was now a far cry from how it had looked while he and Annie had been growing up.

In his mind's eye he could still see the antique stove his mother had somehow coaxed into working long beyond the time it should have. If he tried hard enough, he could make out the shadow of the battered pine table where he and then Annie had done their school-work. The same table where the family had gathered at suppertime for loud long discussions on everything from the Chicago Cubs to Darwin.

Jake blinked, and in place of that old familiar table was the heavy Santa Fe style polished-oak dining set Linda had purchased three years before. He frowned thoughtfully. True, the ranch hadn't had much in the way of comforts when he was a kid. But there was always enough love.

The one thing his new and improved ranch house lacked.

Jake shook his head and reached for his coffee cup. He took one last drink of the still-hot brew, then slammed the cup back down onto the counter. Keep your mind on business, he told himself. Thoughts of love and what-might-have-beens wouldn't get his work done.

And thoughts of Linda would only give him an ulcer.

"Besides," he said aloud into the empty room, "you've got to check the fencing before nightfall." With the rain and the howling wind, he couldn't risk wires coming down and his stock wandering out onto the roads.

Besides, if the weatherman was right for a change and the first snow of the season was really headed in that night, then he'd best keep ahead of the chores.

He snatched his rain slicker and hat from the pegs near the back door and pulled them on, purposely keeping his back to the shiny sterile room. The sooner he was started, the sooner he'd be back. With a microwaved pizza, a beer and a front-row seat for the football game on TV.

If he kept the volume loud enough, he just might be able to convince himself that he wasn't really lonely.

"I know just how you feel," Casey told the little animal, and reached down to grab another handful of wet white lace. Draping the fabric across the calf's shivering body, she hovered over him, blocking most of the rain with her back. She stroked his neck and looked into his sad brown eyes. "It's no fun being cold and wet and alone, is it, pal?"

The calf snorted.

"Gesundheit," Casey said automatically, then blew fruitlessly at a sopping-wet lock of blond hair hanging in front of her right eye. She didn't want to let go of the calf long enough to shove her hair and what was left of her veil off her face. The poor little thing was so scared it would probably take off, and she'd never manage to catch it again, running in the mud.

The trembling calf shifted position, leaning into her. She staggered under its surprising weight and looked back into those big brown eyes. "Do you know something? Your eyes are a lot like my fiancé's. Or rather, my ex-fiancé's." She frowned slightly before adding, "But don't worry, I won't hold that against you. They look better on you, anyway."

The animal snorted and bawled again.

"I felt like crying myself earlier," she murmured sympathetically. "You might not know this, but I was supposed to get married today."

Her little friend shivered heavily.

"I know. It gives me cold chills just to think about it now." Casey leaned down and rubbed her cheek against the back of the animal's head. Her feet felt like two blocks of muddy ice and she was beginning to lose feeling in her fingers altogether. Stupid weather. Trying to ignore her own discomfort, she kept talking to her little friend. "The worst part was telling everyone that there wouldn't be a wedding. You should have seen their faces, pal."

He mooed quietly.

"Who?" she asked with a choked laugh. "The people in the church, of course." She sniffed. "And my parents. It's a good thing for Steven that his note said he was going to Mexico. If my father had been able to get his hands on that jerk…" She sighed and lifted her head to look at her new friend again. "It's not every day a girl gets jilted, you know. Don't you think I should be feeling worse than I am about all this?"

The calf shook its head.

"I don't, either," Casey's fingers stroked the animal's rough yet smooth hide. She shivered hard before saying, "Now don't be offended because I said your eyes were like Steven's. It's not your fault, after all. Besides," she pointed out with a wry smile, "you seem to have a much more pleasant personality."

The calf moved and stomped on her toes.

She yelped and dragged her foot out from under the animal's hoof. "You dance like Steven, too."

The wind kicked up, snatching at her veil and flinging it out around her. "I know it's hard to believe now," she told the squirming calf, "but a few hours ago, I looked pretty good."

An image leaped in her brain. Of her, standing at the back of the church, waiting for her cue to start down the incredibly long pine-bough-decorated aisle at her father's side. She'd looked at her ten maids of honor lined up in front of her and realized she didn't really *know* any of them.

Oh, they went to the same functions. Told the same stories. Laughed at the same jokes. But not one of those ten women would she have considered a friend. Then it had struck her that the one real friend she had wasn't even attending her wedding. Annie had refused to watch her friend make what she called a "giant mistake."

The doubts she'd been battling for months had risen in her again. But then the organ music had started, swelling out into the church and stealing away her breath. The first bridesmaid had been about to start her staggered walk down the aisle when an usher had brought Casey the note from Steven.

During the next few interminably long minutes, she'd endured curious stares, hushed whispers and even a muffled laugh or two. She hadn't been able to find a friendly face anywhere in the crowd of surprised disappointed guests.

Even her parents had been too stunned to offer comfort to her. Her father, grim-faced and tight-lipped, stood awkwardly patting her mother's shoulder as she wept quietly into her hanky. The twins, Casey's older brothers, looked as though they just wanted to find someone to punch.

Naturally, when she ran out of the church a few minutes later and jumped into her sports car—which one of her brothers had thoughtfully driven to the church—she'd instinctively headed for her one real friend.

The only person she could count on to listen to her.

To tell her that she wasn't crazy. That she was right to feel as though she'd just escaped from prison.

Annie Parrish.

Casey yanked her full skirt a little higher over the animal's back and told herself that all she had to do now was find the Parrish ranch. Hopefully before she froze to death. It had been only five years since her family had moved out of Simpson. Why did everything look so different?

The rain, she thought. She was only disoriented because of the rain. When the storm passed, she would find the ranch. *If* the storm passed, her mind added silently. She glanced up at the black clouds overhead, noted the wind-whipped trees surrounding the meadow and fought down her first thread of worry. For all she knew, it could start snowing any minute. By morning she would be nothing more than the ice statue of a haggard-looking bride.

The Irish lace and ivory silk dress she wore felt as though it weighed five hundred pounds. The fabric had soaked up the rain like a dime-store sponge, and the heavy mud along the hemline wasn't helping the situation any. Idly she wondered what the gown's designer would say if she could see her creation now.

The world's most expensive tent for water-logged calves.

And what, Casey asked herself, would her father say?

She groaned quietly and closed her eyes for a second or two. Henderson Oakes wasn't going to be a happy man for quite a while. No doubt he would take Casey's being jilted as a personal affront. Though basically good people, her parents were far more concerned about how things looked than with how things really were.

Better not to even think about them yet.

The rain came down harder and began to feel like a thousand cold knives stabbing her body. Her back ached from hunching over the calf. Her arms were scratched from clawing her way through barbed wire to rescue the little beast. She'd lost one shoe to the muck and she definitely felt a cold coming on.

With any luck it would develop into pneumonia.

"Here comes the bride," she sang softly, then stopped abruptly. If she wasn't so blasted tired and if she wasn't afraid she'd sink neck deep in mud, Casey would have plopped right down on the ground and had a good cry.

"What in *hell* are you doing, lady?"

The deep gravelly voice seemed to come out of nowhere. She jumped, staggered and fell across the calf's sturdy little body. Throwing one hand down onto the muddy ground, Casey broke her fall and ignored the tiny twinge of pain that shot through her wrist. She cocked her head to one side and looked through her veil's saturated netting at a man on a horse.

Finally. Help.

At least she hoped it was help.

She really had to start paying more attention to her surroundings. She'd been so wrapped up in her own thoughts she hadn't even heard the horse and rider approach.

Pushing herself upright, Casey kept one hand on the calf and looked at the man carefully. His hat was pulled down low on his forehead, and an olive green rain slicker covered the rest of him, except for his lower legs and the worn boots shoved into stirrups.

The rain continued to pound relentlessly around them and Casey lifted one hand to shield her eyes, hoping for a better look at the cowboy.

"Cassandra Oakes," he muttered. "I don't believe it."

The obvious displeasure in his tone struck a chord of memory within Casey. How many times had she heard that same raspy voice say, "Get the hell away from me!"? And how many of her dreams had that same raspy voice invaded?

Goosebumps that had nothing to do with the rain and the cold suddenly leaped up on Casey's arms, then raced across her shoulders and down her spine.

Only one man could have such an effect on her.

Even if it *had* been five years since she'd seen him.

Five years since he'd broken her heart.

"Hello, Jake."

Two

Hello, Jake?

That was all she could say? Standing in the middle of his field in a soaking-wet wedding gown, hovering over a mewling calf, and she says, "Hello, Jake"?

A groan rattled through him. When Jake had spotted that convertible on the side of the road, he'd figured someone was in trouble. That road only led to his and Don Wilson's ranches, so there never was much traffic on it. Jake had expected to find some tourist lost in the storm or someone on their way to Don's place.

He sure hadn't expected a bride.

Let alone this *particular* bride.

Man, a day could really go to crap in a hurry, he told himself. Not twenty minutes ago he'd been feeling great. He should have known it wouldn't last. But dammit, he never would have guessed that it would be *Casey* showing up out of nowhere just in time to ruin his good mood.

Ruefully, though, he admitted that her appearance did make a sort of karmic sense. He mentally bowed to the inevitable and asked, "What the hell are you doing here, Casey?" His gaze swept over her ruined bridal gown quickly. "Looking for a church, are we?"

"Running *from* a church, actually."

"Uh-huh." He leaned forward in the saddle. "And where'd you bury the groom?"

"It's a long story." Her face paled a bit.

"Naturally."

Tipping her head back, she managed to swing her soggy veil out of her face long enough to look at him. Those green eyes of hers locked onto him, and Jake felt his insides tighten into knots.

"I'll tell you all about it later," she said stiffly. "But right now, would you mind helping me?"

No one should be able to look that good covered in mud, he thought absently. Then when desire began to rear its ugly head, he heard himself ask gruffly, "Help you what?"

"Save him." She wagged her head at the calf still cradled in her arms.

No animal had looked less in need of saving. In fact, Jake admitted silently, he wouldn't mind trading places with the damn thing. But he remembered clearly that even years ago, she'd had a soft heart for animals. He chuckled slightly as he recalled the year she'd realized hamburgers actually came from cows. She'd been horrified. Probably came from living in town all her life. Hell, the only time she or her brothers ever even saw an animal up close was when they came out to the ranch. Their parents had never allowed their children to have a pet of any kind.

Her brothers. Jeez, it had been a long time since Jake had seen the twins. Of course, between working twenty-five hours a day on the ranch and his brief but memorable marriage to Linda, he hadn't had time for any of his old friends.

"Jake? Earth to Jake."

"Huh?" He frowned and forced himself back to the problem at hand. "Oh, yeah. The calf. Save him from what?" He was too wet and cold and tired to be dealing with this. He'd learned long ago that when talking to Casey, it paid to stay alert. Even then, it often wasn't enough.

"He's scared," she said.

"Scared?" Jake's fingers tightened on the reins. Knowing he would regret it, Jake heard himself ask a question, anyway. "And just what is he scared of?"

"The storm, of course."

The wind howled through the trees as if to underline her statement, and the calf squirmed against her. Casey's eyebrows lifted and she nodded shortly as if to say, "See?"

Jake's teeth ground together. She was as stubborn as ever. And as beautiful, his brain added, even with her hair hanging in limp soggy strands along her cheeks. Even with her wedding dress splotched with mud. Even with her emerald eyes squinted against the downpour. Uneasily Jake watched her widen her stance and wiggle her behind as she struggled to get a better grip on the animal.

Something hard and tight settled in his chest, wrapping itself around his lungs and heart. He struggled to draw a breath. Even after five years she still had the same old effect on him.

For the first time since leaving the ranch house, he was beginning to wish his Jeep wasn't out of commission. At least then he'd be seated on a nice comfy bucket seat, instead of futilely trying to find a comfortable position in the saddle. Dammit. He'd always enjoyed riding in the rain.

Until now.

Immediately he told himself to get a grip. She was wearing a damned wedding gown. She'd said she was running from a church. But she hadn't said whether she'd started running before or *after* the wedding.

The notion of Casey's being someone else's wife tightened that cold band around his chest another notch.

Rain pelted his hat and slicker. He felt the slap of each drop and welcomed it. At least he knew what to do about rain. *She* was another matter entirely.

"Are you going to climb down and help me or not?"

Jake shook his head, tightened his grip on the reins with one hand and rubbed his jaw viciously with the other. There was no way he'd be able to climb down from his horse and walk. Even if his rain slicker did hide his body's reaction to her, his discomfort would be all too visible.

But he had to do something.

This ridiculous conversation was getting them nowhere.

"Cows *live* outside," he said.

The calf bawled piteously.

Casey cooed in sympathy, then flashed Jake a hard look. "He's just a baby."

"Who weighs more than you do."

A deep reverberating sound rolled out around them

and Casey half straightened, still keeping her arms around the animal beside her.

"What was that?"

"That would be his mama, I'd bet," Jake told her when she swiveled her head to look at him.

The calf called a quavering answer and its mother mooed back.

"Here she comes," Jake said, and dipped his head toward the distant line of trees.

She looked in the direction he indicated and sucked in a quick breath. Mama indeed. A huge cow was lumbering toward her, moving much more quickly than Casey would have thought possible. Apparently her friend didn't need saving as much as *she* did at the moment. Immediately she released the calf and started for the man and relative safety.

She grabbed up fistfuls of skirt, hiked the hem past her knees and trudged through the mud. The cow's hoofbeats pounded against the sodden ground and sounded like native war drums to Casey. It seemed to take forever to cross the few feet of space separating her from the horse, and naturally Jake wasn't offering the slightest bit of help.

Just as that thought raced through her mind, though, he urged his mount closer, kicked free of a stirrup and held out one hand to her.

She looked up at him and didn't see even the tiniest flicker of welcome in his blue eyes. She hesitated, glanced over her shoulder at the approaching two tons of offended motherhood and chose the lesser of two evils.

Slapping her hand into his, she felt his long callused fingers fold around hers in a firm grip. Ignoring the warm tingle of awareness sparking between them, she stuffed one muddied stockinged foot into the stirrup and allowed him to pull her up behind him on the saddle.

Immediately Jake turned his horse around and kneed it into a fast walk. After a few feet he pulled back on the reins, bringing the horse to a stop. He turned in the saddle to look behind him, and she shifted to follow his gaze.

She smiled as she watched the calf dip its head below its mother's belly and nuzzle around for milk. Of course, the cow still didn't look very happy with the two interfering humans, but at least Casey's young friend was safe.

And so was she.

"Here," Jake said, and dropped his hat onto her head.

She tipped the brim back and looked at him.

Rain flattened his thick black hair to his skull, and he reached up to brush it out of his way. His blue eyes were hard as he stared at her, but there was a spark of something else there, as well. Then in a heartbeat it was gone.

"I'll take you to your car."

"Don't bother," she told him, remembering that loud snap when she'd stomped on the brakes. "I think it's broken down."

"Perfect," Jake grumbled, and turned the horse's head. "Wrap your arms around my waist," he said. "It's about a ten-minute ride to the ranch from here."

"What about my car?" She pointed at the abandoned convertible.

Jake frowned and spared the car a quick glance. "We can call for a tow from the house."

When the big animal beneath her jumped into a canter, she jolted backward into nothingness. Quickly she reached for Jake and folded her arms around his hard flat stomach. Scooting in closer to him, she pressed herself against his back and felt his muscles bunch beneath her touch. A warm curl of something she hadn't allowed herself to think about in five years began to thread its way through her body. She squeezed her eyes shut. She'd thought those feelings were gone forever. Lord knew, she'd worked hard at forgetting them.

But apparently she hadn't worked hard enough. Here she was, less than ten minutes with the man, and her knees had turned to rubber. Maybe what she should do was dredge up that memory of the last time she'd seen him. Remember the embarrassment. The humiliation. Surely that would be enough to quell whatever lingering feelings she had for the man.

No. Immediately her mind rejected the plan. She wasn't going to relive that night again. Not for any reason. Not if she could help it, anyway. Besides, she told herself, her reaction to Jake no doubt had more to do with her already emotional state than with the man himself.

She was so cold. So tired. She thought about resting her head on his back, but then reconsidered. No sense racing out to meet problems with open arms.

Deliberately she sat up straight and loosened her hold on his waist a bit. Instead of letting her mind wander down dangerous paths, she concentrated on moving with the familiar rhythm of the horse's steps. Years of riding lessons at exclusive stables were finally paying off.

Jake sucked in a gulp of air and she thought he muttered something.

She shifted to one side, tipped her head back and asked, "What did you say?"

"Nothing," he snapped. "And sit still, will you?"

He dropped her off at the back door to the house, then took his horse to the barn. In no hurry to join the woman waiting in the kitchen, he took his time in unsaddling his mount and drying him off. Only when the horse had been fed, watered and put away for the night did he step to the open doorway and look across the open ground at the house.

Bright light spilled out of the windows, layering the ground's puddled water with brilliant splashes of color. He turned his head to look at the guest house, two hundred yards away. The lights there were off but for a single lamp left burning in what he knew was the living room. The blue Ford pickup was gone from the front of the house.

So, the foreman and his wife had gone into town despite the storm.

That left him and Casey entirely too alone for comfort.

And he couldn't get rid of her anytime soon, either. With his Jeep not working and the pickup gone for who knew how long, they were stuck together.

Dammit, why did she have to show up here? And why was she still able to take his breath away with a single glance?

Grumbling at his own foolishness, he stepped out of the barn, shut the double doors behind him and walked into the wind and rain. He crossed the yard slowly, as if hoping the cold would erase the spark of heat she'd created when she'd wrapped her arms around him. But it didn't help. The fire in his blood remained, and as he recalled the feel of her legs pressed along his own, his body tightened uncomfortably. Halfway to the house, he stopped dead and tilted his head back to glare at the stormy sky.

Hard heavy rain pummeled his face and chest. A cold fierce wind rushed around him, tugging at his coat with frigid fingers. He squinted against the icy pellets and noticed an occasional spot of feathery white drifting down toward him.

Perfect.

Snow.

"What did I ever do to you?" he demanded hoarsely of a silent heaven.

The snowflakes thickened amidst the raindrops.

Jake straightened, shook his head, then loped across the muddy ground to the back porch. He stripped off his slicker and snapped it in the air, shaking off most of the water. Then he dropped it onto the closest chair, stomped the mud from his boots and opened the door to meet trouble face-to-face.

She was standing in front of the kiva fireplace staring into the flames still dancing across the logs he'd laid earlier in the afternoon.

"You're shivering," he said lamely, and she turned to look at him.

"I'm warmer than I was."

Maybe. But her teeth were chattering. His gaze

swept over the sodden once-beautiful white dress, and he wondered again about the mysteriously missing groom. What kind of idiot would let a woman like this escape him at his own wedding?

Wet fabric clung to her like a determined lover, outlining her small breasts and the curve of her hips. What should have been a full skirt now hung straight down her legs, wrapping her in a blanket of muddy lace.

A sharp pain pierced his chest as he let himself actually think about her being married to someone else. But in the next instant he buried the pain. What was done was done. He'd made his decision five years ago and he still believed it had been the right one.

No matter *what* it had cost him.

He lifted his gaze to hers, pushed both hands through his wet hair and said gruffly, "What are you doing here, Casey?"

She sniffed, snatched her veil from her head and twisted it between her hands. Dirty water streamed from the sodden netting. "I came to see Annie."

"Oh." His sister. He nodded. Of course she was there to see Annie, you idiot. Why in hell would she have come to see *him?* He inhaled deeply, blew the air out of his lungs with a rush and said, "Annie doesn't live here anymore." At her questioning look, he added. "She moved back to town about six months ago."

"Stupid," Casey muttered, and gripped her soggy veil more tightly. Shifting her gaze back to the fire, she said, more to herself than to him, "I should have known that she'd want to be back out on her own as quickly as possible."

She darted a quick look at him and he saw disappointment shadowing her eyes.

"How's she doing?"

"Pretty well." He lifted one shoulder in a half-hearted shrug. "You know Annie. Divorce is hard on anyone, but she'll be OK."

"I know she will."

"Yeah. I made it. She will, too."

"That's right." She straightened slightly and turned those green eyes on him. "Annie told me about your divorce. I'm sorry, Jake."

Discomfort rattled through him briefly as he looked into her eyes and saw sympathy and understanding. He shifted uneasily under her steady regard and wished she would change the subject. He didn't want to discuss Linda with her or anyone else. In fact, except for the valuable lesson Linda had taught him, he preferred to forget all about her.

"It was a long time ago," he said.

"Not so long. Only three years."

His gaze narrowed. Hell, he hadn't seen Casey in five

years, but apparently his little sister kept the woman up to date on his life. "Is there anything Annie left out?"

"Not much," she admitted.

"Remind me to have a talk with my sister, huh?"

"How's Lisa?"

A small smile erased Jake's frown. Happened every time he thought about his three-year-old niece. It was simply impossible *not* to smile when thinking about the little terror.

"She's great. Driving Annie nuts."

For a too-brief moment Casey's smile joined his. "I haven't seen her in so long I probably wouldn't even recognize her." Her smile faded. "What about Lisa's father?"

He stiffened and unconsciously his hands curled into fists. As thoughts of Lisa could bring a smile, thoughts of her no-good father gave birth to sudden bursts of rage.

"Like you, he's been gone so long he wouldn't know his own daughter. Unlike you, he wouldn't care."

"That's a shame."

"Among other things."

Long silent minutes passed, and the only sounds were the rain drumming on the tiled roof and the snap and hiss of the fire. Finally Casey broke the tension-filled quiet.

"I don't suppose you could give me a ride to town?"

"Can't."

"Why not?"

He frowned and shook his head. "Jeep's broken down and my foreman used the pickup to take his wife dancing. From the looks of this storm, they probably won't make it back until morning."

She stared at him as if she couldn't believe what he was saying. Well, he wasn't thrilled with the situation, either. She would just have to get used to it.

"Surely you have more than one Jeep and one truck on a ranch this size."

"Well, now," he drawled deliberately, "I surely do, ma'am. But I'm afraid my city car wouldn't fare any better than *your* car did in this mud."

"Oh."

"Yeah, oh."

"Can this day possibly get any worse?" she muttered.

"It's snowing," he offered.

A short strangled laugh shot from her throat. "Of course it is."

He watched her as she began to rub her hands briskly up and down her arms. As he stood there, a violent tremor rocked her. He felt like an idiot. While he was questioning her, she was no doubt catching pneumonia.

"You're never going to warm up while you're wearing that."

Her perfectly arched brows lifted high on her forehead. "Why, Jake," she said. "Are you trying to get me undressed?"

"Knock it off, Casey." He headed for the stove where he picked up the teakettle and carried it to the sink. As he filled it with water, he told her, "We've known each other too long for this. Just get out of the damned dress. You know where the bathroom is. I'll find you a robe or something."

When the kettle was half-full, he carried it to the stove, slammed it down on one of the burners, then turned on the fire underneath it. Then he stomped out of the kitchen without waiting to see if she was following his orders. The truth was, he admitted silently, he sure as hell didn't want to be anywhere near her when she started peeling off that dress. His little sister's friend or not, what she was doing to him was downright dangerous.

He marched down the long hallway to his bedroom at the back of the sprawling adobe-and-wood house. Throwing the door open, he absently noted the crash as the heavy oak panel hit the wall. But he was on a mission. Find something concealing for her to wear. Yes, he thought. Definitely concealing.

A burlap bag with a matching hood should do the trick.

Unfortunately he told himself as he stepped into the bathroom and glared at the garment hanging from the hook on the back of the door, all he had was a terry-cloth robe.

And a *short* robe at that.

Doesn't matter, he thought grimly. The important thing here was to get her dry. Then he'd dig out an old pair of sweats or something. Somehow, he had to survive the night, then get her the hell out of his life.

Again.

Clutching the robe in one fist, he marched back into his bedroom and came to a sudden stop at the foot of his bed.

In the past five years many things had changed. For one, he now slept in the master bedroom, not down the hall in the room where he'd grown up or even the guest house where he'd lived for a few years. He had changed most of the furnishings, painted the walls, installed new drapes. But the huge four-poster was the same. The same bed he'd slept in all his adult life.

And the same bed he'd found Casey in one night five long years ago.

Instantly the past was all around him, and he shuddered with the force of the memories.

There'd been a party in town. Casey's brothers had thrown themselves a farewell get-together. Since the

Oakeses were leaving Simpson for the relatively big city of Morgan Hill, they'd decided to stage one last event for their friends.

He had left the party early, hoping to find some peace and quiet before his parents and sister returned to the ranch. He'd been living in the guest house then. A consideration, his father'd called it. A necessity was how Jake had thought of it. Even though working the family ranch was all he'd ever wanted to do, a thirty-year-old man needed more privacy than living in his parents' house could afford.

He'd walked through the dark guest house, not even bothering to turn on a lamp. In his mind, he could still hear the echo of his own footsteps in the empty rooms. He remembered feeling a little sorry for himself that the twins—and Casey—were moving away.

In his bedroom he'd plopped down onto the mattress to tug off his boots. He'd gotten one off and had just started on the other when her voice stopped him.

That so familiar voice had sounded different that night. Throaty, deep, filled with unspoken promises and just a quavering hint of nerves.

"I think you should know you are not alone."

Three

Jake had jumped to his feet, taken two quick steps to the bedside table and fumbled for the lamp switch.

Soft light dazzled the darkness, spilling over the woman waiting in his bed. Propped up with pillows behind her back, Casey lay beneath the covers. The sheet-topped quilt folded neatly across her breasts, she displayed just enough creamy flesh to let him know she was naked.

Jake drew one long unsteady breath, then deliberately took a step away from the bed. "What are you up to?"

She looked at him, then let her gaze slide to one side nervously. "Jake, I—"

"How did you get in here?"

"Annie gave me a key."

"Annie?" Damn, his little sister was in on this! Was this setup some kind of a joke? But no. Instinctively he knew that whatever else she was up to, Cassandra Oakes wasn't kidding.

He flashed her another quick look and had to swallow back a groan. Her long blond hair lay across her shoulders and bare arms. Her green eyes shone with a passion he hadn't expected and didn't know quite how to handle.

Oh, he knew how he'd *like* to handle it. For months he'd been noticing his younger sister's friend—much to his disgust. God, he'd known Casey since she was ten! She was just a kid. At least he'd always thought of her as one. And yet lately, every time she showed up at the Parrish ranch, he was drawn to her. He'd found himself looking for her, hoping to see her.

And that worried him.

Hell, he was thirty years old. He was ready to settle down. He'd been to college. He'd had a chance to taste the rest of the world and had finally realized that the life he wanted was here. On the ranch.

But Casey Oakes was only nineteen—and barely out of high school.

What did she know about life? Or herself, for that matter? She didn't need *him* cluttering up her future just when it was beginning to open up in front of her.

So he had made up his mind to keep his desires in check. To keep a watchful distance from Casey until she'd had a chance to explore the world a bit.

But he'd never counted on having her ambush him in his bedroom.

"You'd better get out of here," he said past the hard knot of need lodged in his throat.

"But I've been waiting for you," she said. Jake watched as she held the covers to her and came up on her knees. She looked at him and shook her hair back away from her face.

He dragged a short harsh breath into straining lungs. Almost unwillingly his gaze shot to the swell of her breasts, where her armor of quilt and sheet was beginning to dip. Every breath she drew tantalized him, pushing him closer to the limits of his own endurance. His palms itched to cup her breasts. He could almost taste her sweet warmth.

Deliberately he clenched his hands at his sides and let his angry frustration color his voice.

"Well, now that I'm here," he said, "you can go."

"No."

"No?"

"Oh, Jake…" She leaned toward him, unknowingly letting that quilt drop another inch or two until the tops of her breasts were bared to his view. She held out one hand to him. "Don't you see? I've wanted this to happen for so long—and now we're moving away. I don't know when I'll be back."

That had occurred to him, as well. In fact, it was the main reason he'd left the party early. He hadn't felt like celebrating the fact that the one woman he was interested in was being spirited out of town. He wasn't a big believer in the old adage "Absence makes the heart grow fonder." No doubt, Casey would forget all about him in a year or two. As would he forget about her.

Which made it even more imperative that he got her the hell out of his bedroom.

"Casey, you shouldn't be here."

"This is exactly where I should be," she countered, and scooted to the edge of the bed, dragging the bedclothes with her. Climbing off the mattress, she walked to him and laid one hand on his forearm.

His skin seemed to burn at her touch, right through the fabric of his shirt. He clenched his jaw tight, determined to ignore the almost electric feel of her so close to him.

"I couldn't wait for you to take the first step

anymore," she said softly, breathlessly. "I'm out of time. I *had* to tell you."

"Tell me what?" Say it, he pleaded silently. Say it and go.

"I love you."

Like a powerful fist to his midsection, Jake felt the blow. He stared into her eyes and saw everything he'd ever hoped to see shining back at him. Lord, how he wanted to tell her the same thing. He wanted to grab her, pull her tightly against him and lose himself in her. He wanted to slide into her warmth and hear her quiet moans of pleasure as they discovered each other. But he couldn't. It didn't matter if she claimed to be in love with him.

Nothing had changed. She was still too young. Too inexperienced to know what she wanted. She was still the kid who had followed him around the yard, peppering him with questions until he'd wanted to lock her in Annie's bedroom.

Despite the fact that she didn't look or feel like a kid at the moment, he couldn't take advantage of her feelings to ease the ache throbbing inside him. And he certainly couldn't expect a kid her age to make some kind of lifelong pledge of love.

Although he thought it might kill him, he forced himself to say, "Thank you, Casey. I appreciate it."

Her eyes mirrored the questions racing through her brain.

"You appreciate it?"

"Casey, I know you don't want to hear this—"

"Then don't say it. Please, Jake." Her fingers curled into the front of his shirt. "Don't say it."

"I have to." He reached up and covered her hand with one of his own. "I'm thirty years old, honey. You're just nineteen."

"I turn twenty next month."

"Twenty, then," he conceded. His thumb smoothed across her knuckles and he felt the warmth of that touch right to his bones. "You haven't even finished college yet."

"What does that have to do with us?"

"There is no 'us,'" he said, despite the pain that statement cost him.

"There could be."

He shook his head.

"Are you saying you don't feel anything for me?" she demanded.

"Casey…"

"I know you do, darn it. I know you feel *something*. I've seen the way you look at me. It's the same way I look at you."

Damn.

"Please, don't turn me away. I don't want to leave you." She stepped closer, reached up and cupped the back of his neck. Slowly she drew his head down to hers, then pressed her lips to his.

Jake groaned and forced himself to stand perfectly still under her gentle assault. The touch of her mouth was electrifying. Something sparked between the two of them. Something rare and magical. Still, he made no move to hold her, instead calling on the strength of his will to resist the incredible temptation she offered.

Then she dropped the quilt and sheet and reached up to wrap both arms around his neck. She pressed herself to him and he felt her hardened nipples rubbing against his chest. Desire rocketed through him, hard and hot. He wanted to do the right thing here, but Lord, he was only human.

When his arms closed around her bare back, a purr of satisfaction rumbled from her throat. His hands moved up and down the length of her spine, touching, exploring. Her lips parted and his tongue swept inside her mouth, tasting her for the first time. She was sweeter, more intoxicating than he had ever imagined. Instantly he knew that if he didn't stop that minute, he would never be able to let her go.

Abruptly he released her and took a step back.

"What's wrong?" she whispered. Her eyes were

glazed with the smoldering fires of a passion just born. It was almost enough to make him forget his blasted attempt at nobility. Almost.

"What's wrong?" he repeated. "This." He bent down, scooped up the quilt and quickly draped it around her. "This whole thing is wrong," he snapped, then took another step away from her.

"How can it be when it feels so right?"

"Damn, Casey! I'm not made of stone, all right?" He glared at her briefly, then stomped past her to stare out the windows at the darkness outside. "Do us both a favor and leave, huh? Now. Before we both do something that can't be undone."

He heard her sniff and knew she was crying. Something cold settled in his chest, but he didn't look at her. He knew that if he turned and saw tears on her face, this hard-won battle would be lost. An eternity-filled moment later she spoke again.

"All right then, I'll leave."

Thank God.

"You're wrong, you know," she said, and he flinched at the pain in her voice. "About us. Age has nothing to do with love, Jake Parrish. And someday you're going to be sorry you sent me away tonight."

The memories ended abruptly as those last whispered words echoed in his mind.

He *had* been sorry.

Every night since.

But especially so tonight.

"So," she asked, "were you ever sorry?"

Jake turned slowly, inevitably, to face the woman standing in the open doorway of the bedroom. She'd finally gotten out of that wet wedding gown and was now draped in an oversize turquoise bath sheet.

"Sorrier than you'll ever know," he admitted finally.

"Good." Casey walked into the room holding his gaze with hers. Strange, the last time she'd been alone with this man she'd been stark naked. Now she wore only a towel. Judging by the flash of awareness in his eyes, he'd certainly noticed.

She'd only had to glance at him to know that he was reliving that long-ago night. Somehow it made her feel better to know that Jake, too, had regrets. She wondered what he would think if he knew her main regret was that she had allowed him to chase her away.

"Here." He held out his robe toward her. "You can wear this while I try to find you some sweats or something."

"Thanks," she said, and took the robe. She slipped into the garment, pulling it on right over the towel already covering her. Once the terry-cloth belt was tied at her waist, she turned back to him.

"I tossed my dress across the shower rod since it's still dripping mud. I hope that's OK."

"Sure."

He looked as uncomfortable as she felt.

History repeating itself?

"This isn't exactly how I imagined my wedding night turning out," she said suddenly on a laugh that held more nervousness than humor.

"What happened?" he asked. "Why are you here and not on some elaborate honeymoon?"

Another choked laugh shot from her throat before she could stop it. "I think the rules are you have to actually be *married* to go on a honeymoon."

His gaze narrowed and even in the semidarkness, she could see his familiar scowl.

Casey reached up and pushed her towel-dried but still-damp hair back from her face. Walking to the bed, Casey perched on the edge of the mattress, bracing her heels on the bed frame.

"What happened, Casey?" he asked again.

She set her elbows on her knees, glanced at Jake and shrugged. "Oh, nothing much. My groom decided at the last minute that marrying me wasn't such a good idea, after all." Her fingers plucked at the robe's worn fabric as she talked.

"He didn't show up?"

How much more humiliation was she supposed to survive in one day? It had been bad enough being jilted. Admitting the facts to Jake was another trip down embarrassment lane. But she supposed she might as well get used to the question. Lord knew she would probably be hearing it from everyone for the next several months.

"Yes," she finally said, "he was there. Long enough to give one of the ushers a note for me."

"A note?" Jake's voice was hard and disbelieving.

She held her breath when he walked to her side and sat down next to her. He made no move to touch her, though, and she didn't know whether she was relieved or disappointed.

"Yeah." She glanced at him and smiled halfheartedly. "It seems Steven suddenly had an urge to visit Mexico."

"Bastard."

"My thoughts exactly," she said, and unconsciously patted his hand. "At least at the time." But now that she thought about it, she was amazed to discover that the anger that had burst into life so swiftly had disappeared again almost as swiftly. Strange. All she felt now was relief—tinged with lingering traces of humiliation.

She hadn't been madly in love with Steven. Now she wasn't sure if she had even loved him at all. She had certainly liked him. Well, at least until today. He was a nice man, from what her mother liked to call a good family. Translation, Casey thought, *rich*.

Their parents had wanted the match and she and Steven had simply drifted into it. She couldn't even recall her ex-fiancé actually proposing. It had simply been taken for granted.

She scowled, lifted one hand and rubbed at her forehead. The mother of all headaches was just beginning to throb.

"I'm sorry, Casey."

"Why?" she asked. "You weren't the one rejecting me this time."

"Let's not go there, all right?"

"Why not?" She turned her head and looked directly into his eyes. The eyes she used to dream about. "This *is* my wedding night, after all. What better thing to at least *talk* about than sex? Or the lack thereof."

"I left the kettle on," he said, and moved to get up. "Why don't we go and get you some hot tea?"

"I turned it off when the water boiled," she told him, and waved him back down to the mattress.

"Casey," he said, and shifted a bit farther from her, "you've had a bad day. Why not just get some sleep, huh?"

"I don't want to sleep, Jake." In fact, she'd never been more awake. Ordinarily she wouldn't have considered seeking him out and asking him about that night—but now that the fates had provided her with the opportunity, she really wanted to know just why he'd turned her away.

He stood up abruptly and began to pace.

"Oh, relax," she told him. "I'm not going to attempt another seduction. You convinced me a long time ago that you weren't interested. I won't ask you twice."

"Huh!" He snorted a laugh and quickened his aimless pacing. "Not interested? I don't remember saying that."

Casey blinked. Swiveling her head, she followed his progress around the room while trying to ignore the sudden flare of heat in the pit of her stomach.

Quickly her brain raced back over the memory of that night. She recalled the feel of his hands on her bare flesh. The taste of his mouth on hers. His strangled breath. But mostly she remembered the gentle yet firm way he'd turned her away.

"Do you mean that you *did* want me?" she asked, her voice hesitant.

"*Want* you?" He laughed shortly. "Oh, I guess you could say that. I could hardly walk for a week."

Casey blinked again. She sat up straighter and half turned to look at him. Standing beside the window, he held the drapes back with one hand and stared out into the night. Flashes of white drifted past the window.

"It's still snowing," she said softly, her gaze locked on his tight features.

"Yeah. Not heavily, though."

"If you wanted me, why did you turn me down?" She had to be crazy. Or at least masochistic. Wasn't being jilted at the altar enough for one day? Did she really *have* to know the answer to that question? Even if it meant adding more humiliation to an already full day?

Yes. She did.

Besides, Jake's rejection was five long years ago. All she wanted now was the reason for it.

When he didn't answer, she repeated. "Why, Jake?"

He glanced at her, his expression stony.

"I had to. You were just a kid." He shifted his gaze back to the snow. "A man just doesn't take advantage of a kid's...crush."

"A crush?" She shook her head at him, but he didn't see her. "I *loved* you."

"You were too young to know anything about love."

"According to who?"

"Me."

"So you decided to be noble."

"I *decided* to do the right thing," he corrected as his fingers tightened on the drapery fabric. "But yeah. I wanted you."

A knot of regret for chances missed lodged in her throat. Her gaze swept over him and she noted that he hadn't changed much in the past five years. Oh, she knew he'd been married. Just as she knew his marriage had been a painful one. Annie had kept Casey up-to-date on him over the years.

But Jake's wanting her?

That was something she was willing to bet that Annie had never known.

God, how she wished *she* had known.

She heard herself ask the next inevitable question. "When did you stop wanting me?"

Jake turned his head and gave her a tight smile. "I'll let you know as soon as it happens."

"You mean...?"

He inhaled sharply, turned away from the window and started for the doorway. "We shouldn't be talking about this," he muttered thickly.

Stunned, Casey scooted off the bed and intercepted him before he could leave the room. Her hand on his arm, she looked up at him, willing him to meet her gaze. At last, clearly reluctantly, he did.

The expression on his face, in his eyes, rocketed through her. Desire. Want. Need. All the old feelings that had burned so brightly between them so long ago were still there. Buried and carefully ignored for far too long, they were alive again now, and there was no way to stop them. Even if she'd wanted to.

Casey swallowed heavily. If anything, those emotions, those feelings, seemed suddenly stronger than ever before. Maybe that long-ago night and even her botched wedding were just foils used by fate to bring them together when the time was finally right.

For one incredible moment she felt as though she'd been given a second chance.

"Jake," she said softly, "I'm all grown-up now."

His gaze swept over her. "I noticed."

She smiled. A skittering of warmth shot from her fingertips, still resting on his forearm, straight to her heart. "I told you I wouldn't ask you again…"

"A wise decision."

"…but I didn't say what my answer would be if *you* asked *me*."

"Casey…"

"I would say…*yes*."

The world stopped.

She knew it had, because her heart wasn't beating and she was still alive. It was as if everything inside her and around her was waiting for Jake's reaction.

Slowly he lifted one hand to cup her cheek. His thumb traced over her cheekbone with tender reverence. She turned her face into his touch and heard his breath catch.

"You're crazy," he whispered.

"Maybe. But I don't think so."

He shook his head. "This isn't about me, Casey. You're just reacting to being stood up. And that's no reason to do this."

"You're wrong, Jake." She turned her face into his palm and left a kiss on his callused flesh. "This has nothing to do with anyone outside this room."

He sucked in a deep breath.

"That night has always been with me," she said softly. "For whatever reason we have a second chance. Tonight." She lifted one hand and covered his fingers, still cupping her cheek. "Maybe you made the right decision five years ago," she conceded. "But whether you did or not, that time is over. Done. For both our sakes make the right decision tonight, too."

Another long moment passed in silence.

"Right or wrong," he whispered as his gaze caressed her face. "This time I'm asking, Casey. Stay with me tonight."

"Yes," she said on a sigh, and rose on her toes to meet his kiss.

Four

Emotion flickered across his features. She thought for one awful moment that he was going to change his mind.

Then his mouth came down on hers in a hard fierce rush of need. There was nothing hesitant or reluctant in his touch. Instead, she felt his hunger as sharply as she did her own. She gasped at the strength of the desire pulsing through her. Five years disappeared as if they'd never been, and once again, Casey was that twenty-year-old girl offering the man she loved everything she had to give.

Only this time he gave back more than she could have hoped.

He parted her lips with his tongue and invaded her warmth with a deep thrust that promised greater delight to come. A shower of sparks ignited inside her at the intimate caress, and she leaned into him, wanting more. He groaned under his breath and reached for the belt of her robe. In one smooth motion he untied the knot and slid the maroon terry cloth down off her shoulders to puddle on the floor.

Casey shivered as his fingers slipped beneath the edge of the bath sheet still wrapped around her. In less than a heartbeat the towel, too, lay on the braided rug at her feet.

Her long still-damp hair hung down her back and she trembled slightly. But then he pulled her tightly to him and his hands began to make swift eager strokes up and down her spine, and her shivering had nothing to do with the chill in the room.

Everything within her responded magically to his touch. It was as if he had reached into her soul and turned a light on all the dark lonely places she had tried for so long to hide. She arched into him, wanting more, needing more.

He groaned and broke their kiss, lifting his head to gasp for air like a dying man. For one long heart-stopping moment he looked at her. She felt his gaze sweep over her nude body like a caress, and any embarrassment she might have felt disappeared under the light of passion glimmering in his eyes.

Suddenly, though, he took a half step back from her, and through gritted teeth asked, "Casey, are you sure about this?"

If she hadn't been sure before, she would have been the moment he touched her. This was right. She knew it. She felt it.

It was five long years since she'd been with him in his bedroom. She had done plenty of growing up in that time, and if he wanted to get rid of her again, it wouldn't be as easy for him now.

"I'm standing here in your bedroom stark naked, and you can ask me that?"

He rubbed the back of his neck as his gaze moved over her again. Thoroughly. "I have to ask. I have to know. I have to know that *you* know what you're doing. This is your last chance, Casey." His jaw tightened and he sucked in a sharp short breath. "If you want to change your mind, say so now."

There it was. His halfhearted attempt to get her to leave. A part of her told her she should take it and run. A voice in the back of her mind shouted for caution. Reason. Logic. But what she was feeling had nothing to do with logic. She took a step closer to him.

"I want you to make love to me, Jake."

He groaned.

"I *need* you to make love to me, Jake." She reached out one hand to touch his chest. He flinched as if burned. "Now."

He yanked his shirttail free of his jeans, then tore the shirt off, sending buttons flying into the shadowed corners of the room.

Her mouth dry, Casey watched as he hurriedly pulled the rest of his clothes off. When he finally stood in front of her completely naked, she sucked in a breath and stared helplessly.

Years of hard work on the ranch had toned his body into a mass of sculpted muscle. His broad chest was tanned, with just a sprinkling of dark hair dusting his sun-bronzed skin. His shoulders looked powerful, his arms strong. Her gaze shifted to follow the narrow trail of dark hair that swept down his abdomen.

She gasped at first sight of his sex. Hard and ready, he looked huge, and just for a moment, doubt leaped into Casey's mind. Then he reached for her and all thought danced out the window to disappear in the softly falling snow.

Cradled close against him, she reveled in the feel of her hard nipples pressed to his chest. She loved the sensation of skin on skin. Warmth to warmth. Hard to soft.

His arousal poked at her belly, and a slow curl of

heat began to unfold between her legs. She moved against him and a low growl of pleasure rumbled from his throat. He dipped his head to hers and once more plundered her mouth. Casey wrapped her arms around his neck to steady herself, then returned his touch with her own. Her tongue stroked his, and a well of satisfaction burst open inside her as his arms tightened around her in response.

As she gave herself over to the delights spiraling within her, Jake slipped one of his hands from her back to smooth over her hip, then slide between their bodies. Her breath caught as his fingertips moved through the nest of blond curls at the apex of her thighs.

Confidently he continued his exploration and smiled against her mouth as she parted her legs for him. As his fingers dipped lower, his other hand cupped her behind and held her steady.

She jumped slightly when he located a single spot of sensation. He groaned and deepened his kiss, silently demanding her attention, her passion. As his tongue thrust in and out of her mouth, his fingers moved over her most intimate flesh.

She trembled violently when a spear of delight lanced through her. Breaking his kiss, she let her head fall back and concentrated solely on the magic in his touch. Her eyes slid shut and bright colors swarmed through the room. Her knees wobbled and she tried desperately to lock them into place. If she moved, he might stop and she knew she didn't want *that*.

As if sensing her unsteadiness, Jake lifted her easily, and carried her the few steps to the bed. Throwing the bedspread to the foot of the mattress with one hand, he eased her down.

Cool clean sheets caressed her back, but before she could enjoy the decadent sensation of lying naked in bed, Jake was there. Everywhere.

As if finally unleashing his passion, he devoured her with his mouth and hands. His lips came down on one of her hardened nipples, and Casey gasped at the almost unbearable pleasure shooting through her. Before she could become accustomed to his mouth at her breast, he dragged his teeth lightly across the sensitive flesh.

"Jake!" She half lifted herself off the mattress, trying to follow him as he shifted position. "Don't stop. Please, don't stop."

"We're just getting started," he said, and gently pushed her back down onto the bed. Dipping his head, he took first one nipple, then the other into his mouth. Using his lips and tongue and teeth, he drove her higher and higher into a world she'd never known existed before.

Casey moved and twisted in his arms, enjoying his attentions, yet craving something she knew lay just out of reach.

She had never known. Never guessed that it could be like this. Jake touched her, and her body turned to fire. Her mind dissolved and coherent thought was impossible. Heat shimmered on her skin, soaking through to her bones and lighting up her soul in a wild inferno of sensation.

The calluses on his gentle hands scratched her smooth flesh, reminding her of his strength. Whisker stubble scraped her breasts, lending another sensation to his lavish kisses.

It was as if he wanted to know every part of her. Feel all of her. Kiss and taste her. His strong fingers explored her body as he suckled and tenderly pulled at her nipples.

Then he lifted his head and she looked up, meeting his gaze boldly.

Desire etched plainly into his chiseled features, he stared down at her with eyes darkened with a passion that only grew stronger as the moments flew past.

She looked wild, abandoned. Her eyes glittered with desire and her lips pouted as if begging to be kissed.

Jake surrendered gladly, taking her mouth with his as if his life depended on it. And at the moment, he admitted, it probably did. He tasted her sweetness and loved her eager response.

He'd been right to turn her down so long ago.

The wait had definitely been worth it.

Her tongue swept over his and he groaned, relishing the electricity that shimmered between them. He had never felt so alive. His body hummed with restless energy and demands he hadn't experienced in far too long. He needed to be inside her. Needed it more than he cared to acknowledge.

Breaking their kiss, he moved to kneel between her legs. Drawing her knees up on either side of him, he looked down at her open pink flesh and rubbed his thumb slowly, deliberately, over the hard nub of her pleasure.

Her body twisted, her back arched and her head tipped back into the mound of pillows behind her. Two fingers slipped into her damp tight heat and she inhaled sharply as if caught unawares. As he continued to stroke her, she planted her feet and lifted herself into his touch. His fingers moved deftly on the most sensitive part of her flesh, and her hips pumped in a wild rocking motion that pushed him nearer the edge of control.

"Help me, Jake," she whispered brokenly. Her fingers curled into the sheet beneath her. "That feels so good," she managed to say on a gasp. "I need…"

"I know, baby," he said, his voice low and strangled.

"I need it, too." Jake swallowed heavily, winced against the pain of his aching groin and moved his hands to cup her behind. He couldn't wait another moment to claim her. To slide into her heat and become a part of her. He had never known such want. Such a desperate longing to join with a woman. To feel her body close around his. To taste her. To swallow her breath and make it his own.

Lifting her hips for his entry, he pushed himself deeply into the warmth he had waited so long to find.

She gasped in pain.

He froze.

Her back bowed.

He cursed.

Her eyes flew open.

Staring into those meadow green eyes, he managed to snarl. "Why didn't you tell me you were a virgin?"

She wiggled her hips, inhaled sharply, then sighed as she wrapped her arms around his neck. "Does it make a difference?"

Deep within her tight hot body, he throbbed for release. The damage was done. There was no going back. Even if he wanted to. Which he didn't.

"Not anymore," he said, and eased his body out of hers only to push his way inside again.

"Jake!"

Her nails dug into his shoulders. Her legs lifted and locked around his hips. He moved and she moved with him. He became caught up in the age-old rhythm, and everything but the need for completion disappeared from his mind.

Sliding one hand between their bodies, Jake found again the tender nub of flesh that held the key to her release. As he stroked her, he watched wonder slowly dawn on her face. Her eyes closed, she bit down hard on her bottom lip and lifted her hips high, arching into his touch, straining.

When the first tremors hit her, she shouted his name and dug her fingernails even deeper into his back. The ripples of satisfaction coursing through her grabbed at him. Her body convulsed and tightened around his, squeezing him until with one final thrust, he emptied himself into her and collapsed like a dead man atop her.

He tried to speak. But first he had to find out if he could still breathe.

A tentative shallow breath of air entered his lungs and he accepted it gratefully. His heart felt as though it was about to burst through the wall of his chest. He knew he should move. He was probably crushing her slender body, but somehow, he couldn't find the strength or the will to lift himself off her.

He'd never experienced anything like that before.

Oh, making love had always been good. Although he hadn't been with a woman in longer than he cared to think about. Ever since Linda, Jake had steered clear of females. Once burned, forever shy.

Still, had it been so long that he'd forgotten how explosive it could be? How incredible?

No. He frowned and finally rolled to one side of her. It wasn't just making love. It was making love with Casey that had made the experience so… He let *that* thought fade away. It was much safer to attack than to sit idly by.

"Why didn't you tell me?"

"Hmm?"

Jake watched her as she stretched and *smiled,* for God's sake.

"I said, why the hell are you still a virgin?"

"I'm not anymore," she replied in a well-satisfied tone. "Thank you very much."

"Thank you?"

"Well, yeah." She shot him a quick confused look. "Sorry, I've never done this before. What is one supposed to say after one has been thoroughly…"

"Ravished?" he finished, scowling at her. "Deflowered?"

She laughed. "Deflowered? Jeez, Jake, you sound like a Puritan!"

Puritan? Him?

"Don't worry, OK? I don't think my father even *owns* a shotgun."

"Casey, you could have told me."

"You didn't ask."

"I didn't think I had to. You had a fiancé. You were getting married today."

"You didn't notice that the dress was white?"

"I didn't think that meant anything anymore."

"Now you know."

He shoved one hand through his hair and stared up at the ceiling. Shadows darted across the open wood beams.

"You should have told me."

"If I had, you might not have wanted to—"

"Damn right," he interrupted.

"See?" She stretched and winced a bit at the movement.

He closed his eyes briefly. Damn. Her first time and he'd treated her like she'd done the deed a hundred times before.

"Did I hurt you?" he asked, already dreading the answer.

"*Hurt* me?" She pushed herself up on one elbow and looked down at him. "It was…wonderful. I didn't know it would be like that at all."

"What were you expecting?"

"Oh, I don't know." She sighed and drew one finger down the middle of his chest. "I suppose I knew it would feel nice, but how could I have expected *anything* as dramatic as that?"

He grabbed her hand and held it tight. Hard to believe, but one simple touch of her finger had his body leaping to life again.

Looking up at her, he studied her fine almost elegant features, the mass of blond hair ruffled around her head like some sort of rumpled halo and the soft shine in her eyes. What in hell was wrong with her fiancé? Why hadn't he married her? And for God's sake, why hadn't he *slept* with her?

Before he could stop himself, he blurted out that last question.

Immediately her features shifted, hardened. She pulled her hand free of his, then flopped over onto her back and crossed her arms over her naked breasts.

"It never came up." Then she stopped shortly, thought about what she'd said and added, "No pun intended."

"I don't get it," he admitted, and levered himself up on one elbow to look down at her. "I didn't think anybody waited for marriage anymore."

"Excuse me for being a dinosaur."

"That's not what I meant."

"If you're thinking I saved myself for *you,* forget it."

"I didn't say that, either." Had talking to Casey *always* been this confusing?

"I came to you once and you made yourself very clear. You weren't interested."

"I think," he said wryly, "that we've pretty much disposed of that notion."

Her lips twitched. "You have a point."

"What'd you say his name was?"

She paused for a moment as if trying to remember what they'd been talking about. Then offhandedly she said, "Steven."

"Steven," he repeated quietly. "The man must be out of his mind."

She drew her head back and turned to grin at him. "Why, Jake Parrish! I believe that is the *nicest* thing you've ever said to me."

His eyes rolled heavenward as he turned onto his back to stare at the ceiling again. "Let's return to what just happened."

"Yes," she agreed, moving to rest her head on his shoulder. "Let's."

"Cut it out, Casey," he warned, and tried to inch farther away from her.

"You can't pretend you don't want me anymore,

Jake," she said, and skimmed one hand down his body toward his already hard arousal.

"Casey, dammit!" He caught up her hand and held it tightly. "You're a *virgin*. My sister's friend. A...a *kid!*"

"Taking your objections one at a time," she said, pausing only to plant a quick kiss on his chest, "as you have no doubt observed, I am not a virgin anymore."

"Lord."

"As to being Annie's friend, of course I am. So what? Everybody is *somebody's* friend."

"Knock it off, Casey," he grumbled as her teeth scraped across his flat nipple, sending shock waves of desire through him.

She lifted her head and smiled at him. "As for the last objection, I think even you have to agree that I'm not exactly a kid anymore, either."

He inhaled sharply, then released the breath slowly, painfully.

Casey smiled to herself. He was weakening. She glanced below his waist. Well, not *all* of him was weakening. Hesitantly she moved to touch him.

He gasped through clenched teeth, and as her fingers curled around him, she felt him shudder. An incredible feeling of power rose in her. Jake Parrish wanted her. He could deny it all he wanted to. His body couldn't hide from her.

Her heart felt full enough to pop. Now she knew why she'd been so relieved when Steven jilted her. Of course she hadn't wanted to marry the man her parents had chosen for her.

She still had too many deep feelings for Jake.

"A *virgin,*" he muttered thickly, disgustedly.

Casey leaned over him, her hair falling over one shoulder to drag gently across his chest. She placed a brief tantalizing kiss on his lips, then lifted her head to look at him.

"Jake, one virgin more or less isn't going to mean the downfall of the nation. You're not a criminal. You didn't tie me down and force me."

At that notion he groaned again.

She grinned. "If anything, *I* took advantage of *you.*"

"What?"

"Sure," she said, warming to her subject. "I seduced you with my wicked city wiles and then had my way with you. You being a poor innocent country boy, you had no choice but to go along."

A reluctant half smile hovered around his mouth.

"Feel better?"

"Maybe," he said.

"Well," she whispered as she bent to kiss his flat nipple, "I have an idea on just how you might *positively* feel better."

"Casey," he said, and cupped her face with one callused hand, "we can't do this again. Once was a mistake. Twice would be downright foolish."

She winced inwardly, but gave him a smile, anyway. "Be a fool with me then, Jake." She leaned over him, dropping soft tender kisses on his brow, his eyes, his cheeks. "Just for tonight be a fool with me."

Five

She held her breath, waiting.

Her stomach fluttered nervously. Her mouth was dry and she was sure that if she held her hands out, she would see them tremble.

Ridiculous. She'd just made love with the man. What was left to be anxious about? But she knew the answer to that question. Their brief passionate encounter had been exactly what her mother used to warn her about. When hormones and desire get out of control, sometimes you do things you wouldn't ordinarily do.

If they made love again, though, it would be because she and Jake both wanted to experience it all again without the wild mind-blurring haze of maddening desire to cloud the issue.

His brow furrowed slightly, then his blue eyes narrowed as he looked up at her.

"What?" she asked.

"Something just occurred to me." He pushed himself up onto both elbows and tipped his head to one side. "You were a virgin and didn't tell me."

"I thought we'd covered that."

"What else didn't you tell me?"

"What do you mean?" What else *was* there?

"Casey, are you…do you…? Hell. Are you on any kind of birth control?"

Oh, Lord. She felt her jaw drop.

"Damn." Jake dropped back onto the bed like he'd been shot.

"I didn't think," she said quickly. "I've always wanted children and Steven said it was up to me." She frowned thoughtfully. Steven hadn't even cared enough to express an opinion about whether or not to have children. She'd never considered preventing a child. For as long as she could remember, she'd wanted a family of her own.

She touched her flat belly and wondered if Jake had just given her the child she'd longed for.

He saw her movement and obviously misinterpreted her expression. "There's probably nothing to worry about," he said. "The chances that you actually conceived on your first time must be pretty slim." He inhaled sharply. "But if you did, we'll think of something."

She lay down next to him again and rested her head on his chest. Beneath her ear, his heartbeat thudded steadily. It was a long moment before he draped his arm around her. When he did, Casey smiled.

"I'm sorry, Casey," he said softly. "It never should have happened. I can't even remember the last time I acted before thinking it through."

"Don't be sorry." She tipped her head back to look at him. "I've wanted this to happen for a long time."

He gave a choked laugh and shook his head. "You don't make it easy for a man to feel guilty."

"There's nothing to be guilty about."

"You might be pregnant," he reminded her, and his hand on her arm tightened briefly.

"But probably not," she said. "You said yourself the chances were slim." Although, she added silently, if it was going to happen to anyone, it would probably happen to her. She had always been *lucky* that way.

"Yeah. Look." He gave her a quick pat, then moved away and eased off the mattress. Standing beside the bed, he said, "We'd better find you some dry clothes. You can stay in Annie's old room tonight. I'll call a tow for your car in the morning."

"Jake—"

"Casey, it's over."

"It doesn't have to be," she said in a rush. She didn't want this time with him to be finished so quickly. For whatever reason, she'd been granted this one night with the man she'd dreamed about for years. And just this once, she was going to do what she felt she *needed* to do. Something for her. Something to hold on to in the nights to come. Something to remember forever.

She wanted this one night with Jake more than she'd ever wanted anything. And this time, she was willing to fight to have it.

"Casey, we can't take another chance."

"Isn't there another way? Something we can do?"

He stared down at her, and in the half-light, she saw the indecision on his features. Steeling herself with a deep breath, she sat up straighter and let the sheet drop from in front of her. His gaze shifted to her breasts, and she watched as lines of strain deepened in his face.

She leaned toward him, extending one hand. "Jake, this is our night. The night we were always meant to have."

"You don't really believe that, do you?"

"Yes. I do." Her fingers trembled and her arm began to ache, but still, she held her hand out toward him.

"For some unknown reason, we were brought together tonight. We would be crazy to turn away from it."

"Dammit, Casey…"

A strong gust of wind rattled the windowpane. She gave him a small smile. "It's a sign."

"It's a storm." One corner of his mouth lifted slightly as his gaze moved over her again.

"Just tonight, Jake."

"I must be out of my mind," he muttered as he knelt on the mattress and gathered her close.

Casey's pent-up breath escaped in a slow sigh, and she melted against him. The warmth of him surrounded her, and she told herself to remember it all. Her breasts flattened against his broad chest. His arms wrapped tightly around her, his breath on her hair, her name sliding from his throat on a whisper.

His lips met hers in a slow languorous kiss as he eased them both down onto the mattress. He tasted her bottom lip, then the top. His teeth nibbled at her mouth, teasing her with a promise of more to come. Casey lay across his chest, a willing captive. He cradled the back of her head, threading his fingers through her hair.

She'd never known that the scalp could be an erogenous zone. But the feel of his fingers against her head sent needles of awareness pricking along her spine.

In one easy motion he rolled over, tucking her

beneath him. He didn't break their kiss. Instead, he deepened it, his tongue caressing, tasting her. She welcomed his gentle invasion and released the last bit of anxiety hiding in one corner of her heart.

She ran her hands across his back, measuring the corded muscles beneath her palms. So strong yet so gentle. His body hovered over hers, covering her, protecting her, enticing her with its very presence. Arching into him, she silently demanded more. She wanted to feel his hands and his mouth on her breasts again.

She wanted to feel it all.

Jake shifted slightly and trailed a line of damp slow kisses along the line of her slender throat. He smoothed his left hand over her body, skimming across her flesh with the leisurely tender touch he should have given her before. Her first time should have been special. Gentle. He couldn't change what had already happened. But he could give her this. Give them both this.

He bent his head to take one of her nipples into his mouth. She gasped with pleasure, which sent identical waves of delight rippling through him—and he didn't dare ask himself why.

Sliding his left hand across her belly, he cupped her center, letting her damp heat touch him, warm him. Something in his chest tightened, threatening to choke off his air. He dipped one finger inside her and groaned at the feel of her body surrounding him. She instinctively drew him deeper within.

As a second finger moved to join the first, he switched his attentions to her other breast, clamping his lips around the hard pink nub and drawing at it gently. She groaned and spiked her fingers through his hair, holding his head to her breast as if afraid he would stop.

His heart pounded furiously and he wanted to tell her that he had no intention of stopping, but he couldn't bring himself to abandon her breasts even that long.

Brushing his thumb gently across the small hard button of her sex, he felt her body jump in response. His heartbeat accelerated, and the throbbing ache in his groin almost drove him to the point of madness. He had never known such need. Such want. Her slender curvy body beneath his hands brought him more delight than he had ever found before, and he wanted to know all of her. Reluctantly he lifted his head long enough to claim her lips with his.

He swallowed her sigh as his tongue darted in and out of her mouth. She met him stroke for stroke. Caress for caress. Her untutored enthusiasm fed the fire raging within him until he thought he might explode.

When neither of them could wait another moment to be joined, Jake reached across her to the bedside table. Yanking open the drawer, he grabbed a small foil packet and slammed the drawer shut again. Hurriedly he provided the protection he should have offered her before. Then he positioned himself between her legs and slowly pushed his way into her warmth. He watched as passion took her. Her head tipped back into the pillows and her eyes slid shut.

"Jake..." she groaned softly, and held her arms out for him.

He had to fight his instinct to move into her embrace. Keeping perfectly still in an effort to control his own overpowering need, he inhaled deeply, reminding himself that this time was for her. Buried deep within her body, he looked down at their joining and gently brushed her most sensitive spot with his fingertips.

She swiveled her hips, and the movement made beads of sweat break out on his forehead. He bit down on the inside of his cheek and concentrated solely on pleasuring her.

Casey threw both hands behind her head and clutched desperately at the feather pillows. She needed something stable to hold on to as her world began to splinter around her. His fingers didn't stop. Didn't slow. Over and over, he rubbed and stroked her center until she felt a helpless wail building in her chest.

She rocked her hips in a frenzied attempt to scale the peak she'd just begun climbing. And every movement drove Jake's hardness deeper within her, tormenting her from the inside.

Her breath coming in short rapid gasps, she opened her eyes and looked at him. His gaze was locked on hers. She couldn't look away. Green eyes stared into blue. A muscle in his jaw twitched, and she realized that the same agony of need piercing her touched him, too.

"Jake," she whispered, and reached one hand out to him.

He grabbed it as though it was a lifeline in a stormy sea. Their fingers laced together, she held on tightly as the first shock wave of delight hit her.

Starting off slowly, it built and built, the pleasure deepening, blossoming until the last soul-shattering spasm shook through her. She heard someone scream, and a small corner of her mind recognized the voice as her own.

Still holding her hand, Jake covered her body with his and rocked his hips against her. Small ripples of sensation continued to throb inside her. His steady thrusts heightened the sensation. She locked her legs around his hips, pulling him deeper, closer. Before she knew it or could prepare for it, another wave of tiny explosions battered her. Casey cried out and felt his breath fan her cheek. She squeezed his hand tightly when he stiffened, groaned and surrendered himself to her.

* * *

She shifted, draped one leg over his and snuggled her head more firmly into the curve of his shoulder. Jake scowled into the darkness and tugged the sheet higher up over her. Then, keeping one arm draped around the sleeping woman, he stared into the darkness.

What in hell had he been thinking?

Disgusted, he admitted that he hadn't been thinking at all. He'd reacted. Like a damn high-school kid who couldn't get a grip on his rampaging hormones, he'd grabbed at what was offered without a thought for the consequences.

She muttered something in her sleep, chuckled softly, then wriggled even closer.

Small electrical charges fluttered through him and he frowned. All right, so it was more than hormones. He had never experienced anything like that in his life. Just touching her set off some sort of chain-reaction firework display. There was more at work here than simple desire.

But he wasn't about to go *there*.

He had done the love-and-marriage thing once. It hadn't worked. No way was he going to try it again.

Still, he admitted silently, there was another problem to consider. He'd taken her virginity, for God's sake. Something he'd always managed to avoid before. Dammit, he hadn't been raised to sleep with a virgin and casually walk away.

Especially when that virgin was Casey Oakes.

Not to mention the fact that there was a chance, however slim, that she could be pregnant.

What was he supposed to do now?

Shaking his head, he shifted his gaze to the windows on his left and tried to clear his mind. Just for the moment. He'd be able to think more clearly if he got at least a couple of hours' sleep.

Stars winked at him from a clear sky. The storm had finally cleared out. Maybe that was a good sign.

"Omigosh, omigosh." Annie snatched the muddy wet wedding dress down from the shower rod and raced with it into the kitchen.

"Mommy," the little girl left behind called out, "I still hafta go potty."

But Annie was on a mission and didn't hear her daughter's complaint. Rushing into the kitchen where her father, aunt and uncle sat around the table waiting for Jake to wake up, she demanded, "Look! Look what I found!"

"For heaven's sake," Aunt Emma said with a sniff. "What on earth happened to that beautiful dress?"

"Where'd you get it?" Frank Parrish asked his daughter.

"In the bathroom," Annie told him. "Hanging over the shower rod."

"Should have left it there," Emma said, lifting one black eyebrow at the trail of mud across the Spanish tiles.

"Wonder why Jake has a wedding dress?" Uncle Harry scratched his chin thoughtfully.

"Don't you see?" Annie dropped the dress into her father's lap and looked at each of her thick-headed relatives one at a time. "*This* is what Jake meant on the phone last night."

"This what?"

She flashed a quick dumbfounded look at Harry and went on, concentrating on her father. "Jake said he'd finally succeeded in getting something he'd wanted for a long time."

"Yeah?"

"This must be it!" Annie brushed a stray lock of hair back out of her eyes and grinned at her dad. "Jake got *married!*"

Aunt Emma's dark brown eyes looked like saucers with spilled coffee in the center.

"Married?" Uncle Harry repeated. "Who got married?"

"Jake."

"Annie," her father warned, "you don't know that for sure."

"Why else would he have a wedding dress here?" She shook her head until another long strand of black hair fell out of the neat bun and lay across her shoulder. "What a rat! Keeping this a secret from us. Why wasn't I invited?"

Frank Parrish ran one gnarled hand over the mud-spattered lace gown. "If he *is* married, how did *this* happen? He tied her to his saddle and dragged her through the mud until she said, 'I do'?"

"Oh, I don't know." Annie turned away and started pacing, a soft smile on her face. "It doesn't matter how it happened. I just want to know who."

"Mommy!"

The shout came from down the hall.

"Lisa!" Annie gasped, shamefaced, and started for the door. "I forgot all about her—and she has to go potty."

Aunt Emma sniffed again. "Potty! *Really.* The child's probably had an accident by now."

"Potty is a perfectly fine word." Annie shot her aunt an annoyed look and not for the first time wondered what her sweet befuddled uncle Harry had ever seen in the sharp-tongued old biddy.

"A child should not be taught to shout in public about bodily functions."

"She's not *in* public. She's—" Annie stopped short. She didn't owe anyone an explanation about how she raised her daughter. Least of all Emma. "Never mind," she said, and hastened her steps.

"Mommy!" Lisa's voice was louder, more demanding. "Who's da lady in da bed?"

Emma gasped.

"What?" Harry asked. "What lady? Where?"

"Uh-oh," Frank muttered, and pushed himself out of his chair. Following his daughter, he headed into the hall toward his son's room.

Emma and Harry were right behind him.

Jake's bedroom door was wide open. A slash of morning sunlight lay across the big four-poster and the two people under the sheets.

Annie skidded to a sudden stop at the threshold and her father crashed into her, pushing her the rest of the way into the room. Behind them, Aunt Emma gasped again. Annie glanced at her. She clutched a church newsletter in her beringed chubby hands and was frantically waving it back and forth in front of her flushed face.

Harry pushed his round wire spectacles higher on his nose and peered over his wife's formidable shoulder.

Lisa, a black-haired, blue-eyed, twenty-five-pound bundle of energy, stood at the foot of the bed, holding her crotch and jumping from foot to foot.

"Morning, son," Frank offered.

"Dad." Jake sat up slowly and looked at the small crowd. "Annie."

"Unco Jake," Lisa demanded again, "Who's da naked lady?"

Just then the naked lady sat up beside Jake, clutching the sheet to her chest like a warrior's shield. She blinked wildly, looked at the people in the doorway, then smiled sheepishly.

"The lady," Annie told her daughter, "is your aunt Casey."

"Can *she* take me to go potty?"

Six

Jake tossed a look over his shoulder at the snow-dusted house behind him. Inside his sister was closeted with Casey, and Lord only knew what *she* was saying. He frowned thoughtfully and hoped that his uncle Harry had been able to keep his aunt Emma from grabbing the phone.

From the moment he and Casey had been discovered together, he'd seen Emma's dialing finger twitching. She could hardly wait to get busy spreading the latest gossip. News of finding Jake and a new bride in bed was good. News of finding Jake and someone else's bride in bed was even better!

Wryly he remembered that when he'd decided to divorce Linda, Jake hadn't had to tell a soul. Emma had taken care of notifying the town. And had managed it all in just under two hours.

"Well, son…" his father said softly. Jake turned his head to look at him. "What are you going to do about this?"

"What is there *to* do?" Defensive. Why did he sound so defensive? He was an adult. So was Casey. It was no one else's business if two consenting adults spent the night together. He scowled and hunched his sheep-skin-clad shoulders. If that was true, why did he feel like a teenager caught on the couch with his hand up a girl's skirt?

"Jake," the older man tried again, "I saw that wedding dress." One gray-flecked eyebrow lifted. "It was white. In my day a white dress meant something."

"Everybody wears white now, Dad." The fact that it actually *had* meant something in Casey's case didn't really have to be discussed. Did it?

"True." The older man sighed. "I guess it would be pretty rare these days to find a woman who'd saved herself for marriage. Of course, it'd probably be just as rare to find a man willing to go along with that decision."

Jake shifted uncomfortably. Casey had waited. Only to have her bridegroom jilt her at the altar. Though this might not be the best time to say that perhaps Casey might have mentioned that she was a virgin. It would only sound as if he was trying to duck responsibility. Hell, it even felt like that to him, and he knew it wasn't true. But whatever he said, judging by the look in his father's eyes, this wasn't going to be an easy conversation.

Just a few days ago the Parrish family had celebrated Thanksgiving. If he had known then what would be happening soon, Jake might have been a little less thankful.

Now, though, he was trying to be reasonable. A man of the nineties.

"Dad, Casey's a big girl. She makes her own decisions."

"So do you," Frank countered. "The right ones, I hope."

What did that mean? Oh, hell, he knew what it meant. No, he hadn't used any protection until after the barn door was open and the horse was frolicking. And all right, yes, there was a chance that Casey could be pregnant because of him. A *slim* chance.

Grumbling under his breath, Jake shifted his gaze to the snow-covered meadow beyond the ranch yard. Ridiculous. He might become a father because of a storm and a lost calf. He leaned his forearms on the top rail of the corral fence and tried to convince himself that there was nothing to worry about.

Frank Parrish sighed again, planted one elbow on the same fence rail and cupped his chin in his hand. "You know that Emma's going to be flapping her gums the minute she gets a clear path to a telephone."

"Yeah." But what did that really matter, Jake thought. He and Casey were two consenting single adults.

"And the fact that Casey ran out of the church and straight into your bed is going to make the talc interesting to a lot of folks."

Jake had a feeling he knew where this was going. He just didn't know how to stop it.

"Your mother..." Frank said.

Uh-oh, his dad was pulling out the big guns.

"She was always real fond of Casey. Thought of her as a daughter."

Hell, he refused to look on this little episode as incest! "She's not, though, remember?"

"As close as she can come without being blood."

True. As a girl, Casey *had* spent a lot of time at the ranch. His parents *had* doted on her. But she was all grown-up now. She didn't need a champion.

"That girl," Frank went on, "is like a part of this family. I won't have her cheaply used any more than I would stand by and watch some man take advantage of your sister."

Frank's mouth thinned into a grim line, and pain

flickered briefly in his dark eyes. Jake knew he was thinking about Annie's useless ex-husband. There hadn't been anything either of them could do to protect Annie from hurt and embarrassment then. Obviously Frank was prepared to make up for that with Casey.

Jake stretched his neck as if he could feel a bow tie tightening around it. Across his shoulders, it was as if the snug fit of a rented tuxedo was already boxing him in.

"There's one way to take the sting out of Emma's gossip-spewing." Frank paused before continuing.

Jake knew what was coming. Blankly he studied the puff of his own breath as it misted in the cold air. He kept himself from speaking because he didn't want to prod his father into saying the words out loud.

He should have known that wouldn't stop him.

"You two can get married."

There it was. Tossed into the open where everyone could stare at it. The imaginary bow tie was strangling him now.

"Married?" Jake pushed away from the fence and shoved both hands into his coat pockets. He swiveled his head to stare at his father's calm determined features. "No thanks, Dad. I tried that once."

Frank didn't say a word. He just looked at his son.

Jake shifted uncomfortably. He hadn't seen that particular flare of disappointment in his father's eyes since the night of his seventeenth birthday. Like other teenage fools before him, he'd been convinced that a celebration without beer wasn't a celebration at all. Unfortunately, after his surprise party, he'd tried to drive himself home. He never saw the tree that jumped out into the road and bit his right fender. All he remembered to this day was the look on his father's face when he'd shown up at the police station to pick him up.

Jake had done everything he could since then to avoid reliving that particular sensation.

Until today.

Uneasily he glanced at the house again. Hell, maybe his father was right. Maybe he *should* ask Casey to marry him. It might be the nineties everywhere else in the country, but as for morality in small-town America, it was generally more like the nineties of the past century. And that wasn't altogether a bad thing. Until it affected him personally.

Still, there was something else to consider. Casey would no doubt turn his proposal down, anyway. So he could do the right thing, avoid shaming himself in his father's eyes and still not worry about embarking on yet another disappointing marriage.

"Well?" Frank asked.

"I'll talk to her." Before he could change his mind, Jake started for the house.

* * *

Casey stood in front of the dresser and ran a brush through her tangled blond hair. Then, in the mirror above the heavy chest of drawers, she glanced wryly at the clothes she'd been given to wear. Jake's oversize sweats hung on her small frame. The ribbed cuffs fell past her wrists and had to be constantly pushed up. The pant legs could be pulled over her feet to serve as slippers.

A real femme fatale.

"What on earth went on yesterday?" Annie plopped down on Jake's bed and sat with her legs crossed.

Casey glanced at her friend in the mirror and lifted both eyebrows.

Annie laughed and held up one hand. "OK, I know what went on. What I can't figure out is *why*."

"I suppose it would really look bad for me if I said I didn't know."

"Look, Case." Annie leaned forward, elbows on her knees. "The last time we talked, you were practically walking down the aisle with—" she paused and pushed the end of her nose up with the tip of one finger "—Steven."

"Yeah, well," Casey said, "I was walking and Steven was running. In the other direction."

"Omigod. Jilted? The bastard *jilted* you?"

"Have you ever noticed what a lovely word that is? Jilted, I mean."

"Lovely?" Annie cocked her head and her long black hair, freed from its knot, swung to one side.

Casey turned around and leaned her fanny against the edge of the dresser. Watching her friend's confused face, she couldn't really blame her. *She* should be confused, too. Strangely enough, though, she wasn't.

It was as if she'd been released from prison to find herself in a wide glorious new world. All right. Steven *was* a nice enough guy, and maybe prison was too strong a word. But when she thought about the quick passionless kisses she and her ex-fiancé had shared and then compared them with Jake's kisses…well, there *was* no comparison.

The day before, she had almost married the wrong man for all the wrong reasons. To please her family. To avoid hurting Steven's feelings. And because canceling the wedding after all the time and money spent on it would have been unthinkable for her.

Today, however, it seemed *anything* was possible. Despite the embarrassment of being caught naked in Jake's bed by his father, of all people.

"I'll never be able to look your dad in the face again."

"I don't think anyone was looking at your face, Casey."

"Oh, God."

Annie chuckled again, got off the bed and walked over to her. "Don't worry about it."

"But your uncle Harry is a *minister.*"

"Ministers have sex, I'm told." She paused and shuddered. "Though the idea of him and Emma together is enough to make me want to take the veil."

Casey laughed and immediately felt better.

"See? Nothing's so bad it can't be cured with a good laugh."

"Hope you feel the same way when you see what Lisa's done to her pretty new dress."

Both women turned to look at Jake, standing in the doorway.

"What's she gotten into?" Annie sounded tired but resigned.

"Can't be sure," he said with a shrug. "But it's black and it looks permanent."

"Ohhh…!" Annie got to her feet. "I'll be back, Case. Don't go anywhere."

"She won't," Jake said.

Casey looked from her friend's retreating form to the cool steadiness of Jake's eyes. "I won't?"

"Not until we talk."

"About what?"

"Our wedding."

The room tilted and Casey grabbed hold of the dresser behind her to keep from sliding out the window.

Jake pried one of her hands free and dragged her over to the bed.

"Married?" She shook her head, then raised her confused eyes to meet his.

"Casey," he said, "Emma's in the kitchen inching closer to the phone every second. Harry and Dad won't be able to hold her down much longer."

"So?"

"So, with that phone in her hand, she's more potent than those tabloids in the grocery stores."

"Gossip bothers you?" Even as she asked it, Casey winced. From the little Annie had told her of Jake's divorce, it hadn't been pretty. No doubt the gossips had chewed on him for months.

"It's not me they'll be talking about this time." Jake started pacing. "I'm old news. But you—" he pointed at her "—are fresh meat."

"Oh."

Casey's big green eyes were fixed on him. His navy blue sweats shouldn't have looked so damn good on her. She was practically swimming in them and still she looked beautiful. He gritted his teeth and ignored the sudden rush of blood to his groin. She chewed her bottom lip. Her delicate features made her appear too fragile to stand up to the tidal wave of gossip and innuendo headed their way. Even though rationally he knew Casey was no spun-glass woman, he couldn't deny the protective urge rising in him.

"Jake, I don't live here anymore. Why should it matter what the people in Simpson say about me?"

"Morgan Hill isn't that far away," he reminded her. "And the Oakes name is well-known."

At the mention of her family, she paled.

No wonder, he told himself. Her parents would not be pleased at being the center of gossip. Jake scowled and turned away. Why did he care? All he'd intended was to ask her to marry him. To do the right thing. Why was he standing here trying to convince her to say yes, when he was hoping she would say no?

That was it. No more. It wasn't his business. If Casey felt she could stand up to Emma and her cronies—not to mention her father, Henderson Oakes—that was up to her. He had done his best. He had offered her marriage.

Lord, he could hardly wait for this day to be over. He rubbed the back of his neck as if to loosen that imaginary bow tie. Hell, he hadn't even had the opportunity to tell his family about the land he'd finally managed to buy. This was supposed to be his big day. He should feel triumphant. Victorious.

Ah, well.

"All right, Jake," Casey said softly.

He turned around to look at her. "All right what?"

"All right, I'll marry you."

The bow tie was back. Strangling him.

Beauty and the Beast.

The phrase leaped into his mind as he watched his bride on her father's arm, moving sedately across the great room toward him. Casey looked beautiful. Her hair fell loose in shining waves beneath a crown of red roses and carnations. Soft filmy white cotton fluttered and swirled about her legs, and he had to admit that he liked this dress much better than the one she'd been wearing the week before.

His gaze shot to the Beast. Henderson Oakes. A man of little humor and even less patience. Grimly, as if under protest, he escorted his smiling daughter toward her groom.

In the front row of chairs Frank Parrish sat beside Emma, who continually dabbed a flowered hanky to dry eyes. On the other side of the makeshift aisle, Casey's mother, Hilary, was dressed to the teeth in raw silk and diamonds. She perched uncomfortably on her chair as if expecting the thing to collapse beneath her perfectly toned and sculpted body.

No wonder Casey hadn't wanted to call her parents until the night before the wedding. Hell, he wouldn't have blamed her if she hadn't called them at all. He even understood more clearly now why she had agreed to this marriage in the first place. Marrying him had to be better than having to listen to those two tell you what a disappointment you were.

Then the Beast was there. In front of him. He placed Beauty's hand in Jake's, then took a long step back, distancing himself from the union.

Tucking her hand in the crook of Jake's arm, Casey turned with him to face Uncle Harry, who was conducting the ceremony. The moment she touched Jake her insides settled down. She felt her parents' disapproving gazes driving into her back. But offsetting their grimness were the combined good wishes of everyone else gathered here at the ranch. And her brothers were on her side. Casey leaned forward and looked at the twin standing beside Jake. J.T. winked at her.

Grinning, she straightened again, glanced at Annie on her left, then focused on the minister.

Watery sunshine sifted through the tall front windows, and the scent of fresh pine drifted to them from the decorative boughs hung about the huge room. This small informal wedding, planned and thrown together in less than a week, was, to her mind, more beautiful than the "event" her mother's personal planner had spent four months staging.

A log in the fireplace snapped, and Casey moved closer to Jake. Odd how things worked out. Technically she should have been on a honeymoon in Hawaii with a different groom. Yet here she was marrying a man she'd loved since childhood, despite the fact that he was a reluctant groom.

"I do," Jake said, and his deep voice rumbled through her. Casey blinked and brought her wandering attention back to the business at hand just in time to promise to "love, honor and cherish."

"I now pronounce you husband and wife." Uncle Harry smiled benevolently. "You may kiss your bride, Jake."

He turned obediently to Casey and looked down into green eyes that held far too much optimism. A flicker of regret sputtered to life inside him, then faded again. He had already learned the hard way what marriage was like. It was a shame that he would have to be on hand to watch Casey's education. Almost made a man wish he actually believed in happily-ever-after.

A smattering of applause rose up from their small select audience, demanding the wedding kiss. The light in Casey's eyes had dimmed a bit, and he knew it was his fault for hesitating. Dipping his head, he bent to claim the obligatory kiss. The moment his lips brushed hers, though, obligation flew out of his mind. She leaned into him, tipping her head back. His arms closed around her and he deepened the kiss, parting her lips with a thrust of his tongue. Something fluttered into life in his chest. His blood roared through his veins. Electricity hummed between them. She wrapped her arms around his neck and clung to him. Her tongue met his in a silent dance of promise, and his body's response was staggering.

Absently he heard people cheering and above the raised voices, a wild whistle that had to have come from one of the twins. Lifting his head again, he stared down at his wife and heard his uncle Harry say, "Guess there's no denying this is a love match!"

Love, he wasn't willing to bet on, Jake thought.

But lust, at least, was honest.

"Be honest, Cassandra," her father said. "You participated in this…marriage as a way of saving face. Steven humiliated us and you thought to assuage that somehow."

She swallowed and looked through the doorway into the great room. Everyone seemed to be having a good time. She wished desperately she was out there with them, not standing in the kitchen listening to the lecture she'd known was coming.

"How you could believe that marrying a man you hardly know within a week of being—" her mother lowered her voice, "—jilted would erase public humiliation, I have no idea."

"I've known Jake for years, Mother."

Hilary's eyebrows drew together before she apparently remembered that frowning caused ugly lines. Her features resettled into a familiar expressionless mask.

"Of course, you've known the family. But really, Cassandra, one doesn't simply put aside one fiancé and snatch up another as if they were apples in a barrel."

Casey inhaled deeply.

"I'm certain young Steven would have come to his senses shortly." Her father's voice sliced at her. "There was no need for you to panic."

"I didn't panic," she said firmly. "And even if Steven had come back, I wouldn't have married him."

"Of course you would, dear. Simple misunderstandings are no reason to throw away a perfectly good future. These things happen between couples." Her mother waved a silk handkerchief scented with designer perfume to make her point.

Simple misunderstanding? Being left at the altar in front of a few hundred people could hardly be called a simple misunderstanding.

"I've already spoken to Steven's father. He's going

to straighten out that son of his and then things will be as they should. As soon as we take care of this marriage of yours, Cassandra," her father said briskly. "Which wouldn't have been necessary if you'd bothered to tell us of your plans *before* last night."

That was precisely *why* she hadn't told her parents about her wedding until the night before. In fact, if Jake hadn't insisted, she wouldn't have told them at all until well after the ceremony.

And how typical of Henderson Oakes to attend the wedding and give the bride away, all the while trying to figure out ways of ending the marriage. She'd never doubted that her parents would show up of course. Above all, Henderson and Hilary were concerned with the *appearance* of things. They'd always held the opinion that as long as they looked like a happy family, they were.

"Father," she said, determined to make him listen, "I'm married to Jake now. And that's how it's going to stay."

"Nonsense."

Nothing had changed. But then, why had she expected it to? They never listened. They never heard her. Casey wanted to run into the other room, where dance music issued from the stereo. She wanted to lose herself among the laughing, smiling, dancing people. Distance herself from the people who should have loved her most.

"Casey dear, divorce is simply a part of life." Hilary Oakes waved her hanky again. "Why in even the best of families, divorce has become…commonplace."

"I'll have my accountant contact Mr. Parrish," Henderson said. "I'm sure we can work out a reasonable solution to this and compensate him for any inconvenience."

Casey's fingernails dug into her palms. She concentrated on the physical pain because it was so much easier to bear than her parents' dismissive words. *Inconvenience.* She couldn't help wondering if Jake thought of her as an inconvenience, too.

"Casey?"

She spun around to look at her husband as he walked toward them. Never had she been so glad to see him. He looked wonderful in his tuxedo, even though she knew he hated getting what he called "duded up."

He nodded briefly to her mother, then held out his hand to her father. Reluctantly, it seemed, Henderson Oakes shook his new son-in-law's hand. He opened his mouth to speak, but Jake forestalled him, turning, instead, to Casey. He took both her hands in his and gave them a gentle squeeze. "I came to claim our first dance, Mrs. Parrish."

She blinked, swallowed and blinked again.

It must be the overhead lighting. Making her see

things in his eyes that she wanted to see. Concern. Genuine caring. Perhaps just a hint of love.

But it didn't matter, anyway. Whatever the reason he had come, she was grateful for the rescue.

"I'd be delighted, Mr. Parrish."

Seven

"I moved my things into the spare room," Jake said, and somehow managed to avoid her eyes.

"I don't understand."

Neither did he, completely. All he knew for sure was that vows alone didn't make a marriage. For that, you needed love. He'd learned that the hard way.

Their guests were gone. The few leftovers had been stored in the refrigerator. Most of the mess had been cleaned up. Jake and Casey had been left alone.

And the house was quiet.

Intimate.

"Look, Casey," he said, and shifted his gaze to meet

hers now. Anything less would be too cowardly. "We both know this isn't an ordinary marriage."

"It could be."

One of the roses in her crown had slipped loose of its wire and was lying along the line of her cheek. Her face was flushed with soft color, and near her right breast were raspberry stains in the shape of tiny fingerprints. Apparently Lisa had claimed a dance or two with her new aunt and hadn't bothered to wash her hands first.

Raspberries and Casey's breasts. An intriguing combination.

He stiffened, but ignored the stirrings in his body. He'd be damned if he was going to be led around by his hormones.

"Casey," he said, his voice thick, "let's just see how it goes, huh? Give each other a little room here. Get used to each other."

She cocked her head and he refused to acknowledge the way her soft sweet-smelling hair lay across her throat.

"Why did you ask me to marry you?"

He frowned. "Lots of reasons."

"Give me one," she said, and crossed her arms under her breasts.

Jake's gaze slipped, and before he caught himself and looked away, he thought he saw the dark pink tips of her nipples pressing against the fabric of her gown. How in the hell such a modest dress could suddenly seem so enticing was beyond him.

"Fine," he grumbled. "You might be pregnant."

"Not good enough," she countered. "We'll know for sure about that in a week or two. You could have waited."

"All right, how about my family catching us in bed together?" He bit back a groan at the memory of her smooth skin beneath his hands. For a solid week those memories had taunted him, tortured him. He remembered all too clearly her hushed whimpers. Her moans of pleasure and the tight hot feel of her body convulsing around his.

He felt a hardening in his groin, and he shifted position to lean against the doorjamb. It didn't help.

"Embarrassing," she said, tipping her head back to see him, "but hardly earth-shattering."

"Dammit, Casey!" he snapped. "What the hell difference does it make why I asked you to marry me? I did, you said yes and now we're married. Period."

"It makes a difference, Jake." She unfolded her arms and stepped close to him. "Just like the reason you came to save me from my parents' interrogation makes a difference."

He wasn't sure why he had done that. He'd simply seen her alone, facing down two of the most intimidating people he'd ever known, and gone to help. Protective instincts were just that. Instincts.

"You looked like you could use a friend," was all he said.

"And you volunteered."

"I *am* your husband."

"So you are." She nodded absently, more to herself than to him. Then she ran her hands up his arms to encircle his neck.

"Casey." He stiffened under her touch, summoning up every last ounce of control he could manage to keep from grabbing her and holding her close.

"Jake," she said, and rose on her toes. Stopping when her mouth was just a breath away from his, she asked, "Aren't you curious about why I agreed to marry you?"

"No." Yes, he thought, but not enough to ask. Aloud he said, "Probably for the same reasons I proposed."

"Nope." She brushed her lips across his with a feather touch.

He sucked in a breath and a groan emitted from deep inside him. He curled his hands into fists at his sides.

"It's really simple," she went on, then paused for another brief kiss. "I figured it out myself just this afternoon."

Jake knew what was coming. Even before she said

it, he felt it and braced for the impact of words he didn't want to hear.

"I love you, Jake. Always have." She kissed him again. "Always will."

His hormones stopped sizzling. The flames of desire died as abruptly as if they'd been doused with ice water. Jake stared at her. She sensed that something was wrong. He could see it in her eyes. Slowly her arms slid from around his neck, and she took a single step back.

"Jake?"

"You love me?"

"Yeah."

She didn't sound very pleased about that anymore. Some consolation, he told himself.

"And a week ago," Jake reminded her, "you were going to marry somebody else. Did you 'love' him, too?"

"No."

"But you would have married him, anyway?"

"I like to think I would have said, 'I don't', but we'll never know, will we?"

"We sure won't." He pushed away from the doorjamb and inhaled sharply, ignoring the scent of her perfume as it invaded his lungs. Dammit, he wouldn't allow himself to feel for another woman. To depend on her. They tossed the word "love" around like it was a Frisbee. And the minute a man started to believe it, he was a goner.

Well, not Jake Parrish.

Not again.

If that meant this would be the first platonic marriage on record, then so be it. He'd hoped to reach a compromise of sorts between them. He'd hoped he and Casey could be friends—and lovers. After all, they'd already proved to be mutually satisfying bed partners.

His brain laughed at the weak description of what had happened between them less than a week ago.

But if she insisted on dragging *love* into this mess, he couldn't risk sharing her bed. As much as he wanted to, he wouldn't make love to her unless she understood that he couldn't love her. He wanted nothing more to do with love, thanks very much.

She sucked in a gulp of air and held it. His gaze moved over her quickly, thoroughly. Despite the L-word hovering in the air between them, Jake felt a stirring in his groin again. He might think he knew exactly what he wanted. Apparently his body had other plans.

"Good night, Casey," he said abruptly, and left her while he still had the guts.

Little more than a week later nothing much had changed.

Casey sat at the kitchen table and stared blankly out the window. Her husband was out there somewhere with the foreman. Just as he'd been every day since the wedding, Jake had done everything he could to avoid spending time with her. Even at night, when the chores were finished and they might have had the chance to talk, he sequestered himself in the ranch office. He kept the door to that room, as well as the door to his heart, securely locked against her.

Thinking back, Casey knew the real trouble had started the moment she'd told her new husband she loved him. A wry smile lifted one corner of her mouth. Not exactly the words you would ordinarily expect to start a war.

She sighed and lifted her cup of coffee for a sip. She'd stopped keeping track of how much she'd already consumed that morning, telling herself to enjoy it while she could.

If what she suspected was true, she wouldn't be getting much caffeine for the next eight months or so.

The rich black brew slid down her throat, leaving a trail of warmth for which she was grateful. She felt chilled. Inside and out. December had hit Simpson a few days ago, but even the recurring snow flurries couldn't hold a candle to the icy atmosphere inside the Parrish house.

She'd thought he might be surprised to hear her declaration of love. After all, even she had been taken aback momentarily when the realization struck her. But never had she expected Jake to turn into a tall dark handsome *stone*.

The phone rang and she scowled at it. Infuriating to be interrupted in the middle of a perfectly good pity party.

She snatched the receiver off the hook before it could ring again and snapped, "Hello?"

"Well, hi to you, too," Annie answered, and then had the nerve to chuckle.

"Sorry," Casey said. "I'm not myself today."

"Yeah, I remember how miserable *I* felt this early on."

"Annie…" She never should have said anything. Not even to her best friend. Not until she was sure. And certainly not until she'd talked to Jake.

"So have you done the test yet?"

"No."

"Well, why not? What are you waiting for? A burning bush? A tongue of flame perhaps?"

Casey frowned at the telephone. "If the answer is positive, it'll just create more problems around here."

"Case," her friend said softly, "*not* doing the test won't change anything."

"I know, I know." She reached out and picked up the pink-and-white box she'd purchased at the pharmacy the day before. Gripping it tightly, she said with forced lightness, "Besides, I'm probably not. I mean, what are the odds? About a million to one?"

"About."

"It's not like I haven't been late a day or two before."

"True."

"I'm worried about nothing. Right?"

"Right."

"Liar."

"Coward."

"Okay," Casey said on a sigh, "I'll do the test."

"Now?"

"As soon as I hang up."

"'Bye."

There was a click and then the tuneless hum of the dial tone. Thoughtfully Casey hung up the phone and stared down at the package in her hand.

"The moment of truth," she muttered, and headed for the bathroom.

Jake walked into the kitchen and stopped.

No enticing aroma welcomed him.

His gaze shot around the room. No pots were huddled on the stove. No elegant tempting dessert sat on the marble countertop. Even the coffeepot was empty, though the burner had been left on.

He stepped inside, turned off the coffeemaker, then

looked around the empty room as if waiting for Casey to magically appear. Where was she? For the first time in their short marriage, she wasn't cooking. Surprising how quickly you became used to something. And he'd grown accustomed to hearing the clatter of pots, Casey's slightly off-key yet enthusiastic singing and, especially, the food.

The woman was a Michelangelo of the kitchen. After their wedding, people in Simpson had talked of little else but the meal she'd prepared almost single-handedly. It was no wonder she'd received more than a dozen phone calls asking her—no, *begging* her—to cater small holiday parties.

He snatched his hat off, scratched his head and went into the darkened hall. There were no lights on. Not even in the great room, where falling snow was displayed through the window in Christmas-card perfection. Frowning, he kept moving. Something was wrong.

He snorted a choked laugh at that understatement. What was *right* about their marriage? There probably weren't many newlywed couples who not only didn't share a bed but hardly spoke to each other. His fault, he knew. Casey had tried. But every time he felt himself weakening, wanting to hold her, kiss her, he heard her voice again, saying those three words that were enough to douse even *his* desire.

I love you.

He frowned and hastened his steps. At the end of the hall his bedroom door—*Casey's* bedroom door—stood wide open. He peered into the dusky room, whispering her name. No answer. His chest tightened. What the hell was going on? His gaze shifted. Across the room a slash of light underlined the bottom of the bathroom door. Cautiously he walked toward it.

From inside, he heard her muttering to herself and immediately felt relief wash through him. At least she was all right. Lifting one hand, he tapped gently on the door.

"Jake?"

Relieved beyond words to hear her speaking to him, he said, "Yeah. It's me. Are you OK?"

"Oh, sure," she said, then sniffed. "In the pink."

He frowned slightly. Something in her voice told him there was a problem. He wanted to know what it was.

"Casey? Open up."

"Go away, Jake."

All right. Now he *had* to know what was going on. He tossed his hat onto the bed behind him and faced the closed door as he would any other enemy.

"Casey, I'm not going anywhere until you tell me what's wrong."

She laughed. A short choked laugh that sounded painful.

"Casey, damn it…" He laid one palm against the wood as if he could feel her through the barrier. Worry sputtered into life inside him.

"Oh…"

"Are you going to open the door, or do I take it off the hinges?"

She laughed shortly, and even through the closed door, he could tell there was no humor in it.

"Probably simpler just to turn the knob," she said at last. "It's not locked."

He shook his head, grabbed the knob and turned it. As the door opened, light poured out of the room, and it took a second or two for his eyes to adjust. He saw her sitting on the rim of the tub, staring down at the white plastic stick in her hands.

"Casey?"

"White, no. Pink, yes."

"What did you say?"

"White, no. Pink, yes."

She wouldn't look at him. Her gaze was fixed on that damned stick as if it meant life or death. Irritation simmered inside him. He crossed his arms over his chest and stood there, feet wide apart in a comfortable stance he would keep just as long as it took him to get some answers.

"Why pink, do you think?"

"Pink what?" He tore his gaze from her bent head and glanced around the room looking for clues. Obviously she wasn't going to tell him what was wrong. He would have to find out for himself. He hadn't been in the master bathroom since the wedding. When had she had time to set pots of poinsettias in the terra-cotta window box along the back of the tub?

He shook his head slightly and continued his inspection. It seemed a little strange to see feminine jars and lotions lined up in perfect formation on a countertop that used to hold only a tube of toothpaste and a bottle of aftershave. His gaze landed on an unfolded set of instructions laying half in the sink. Frowning, he reached for it at the same moment she spoke again.

"Since it's pink, do you suppose that means it's a girl?"

He froze, then slowly swiveled his head to look at her.

"No," she argued with herself. "Pink just means pregnant. It could be a boy."

Girl? Boy? His mouth went dry and his brain blanked out. Was she saying what he thought she was saying? No. Of course she wasn't. It was only the one time. What were the odds?

She lifted her head and met his gaze through wide teary eyes, and he knew that odds or not, it was true.

"Congratulations, Jake. We're pregnant." She

sucked in a breath, tightened her grip on that stick and squared her shoulders as if expecting a fight.

Pregnant. Uneasiness warred with pleasure and quickly lost. Delight trounced worry in a flat half second. Happiness battled viciously with anxiety and was clearly the winner.

Moments passed. Two or three heartbeats at most. But in that brief time, he saw at least a dozen different emotions flash across her features. Everything from dismay to joy to a fierce protectiveness glimmered in her watery green eyes.

He dropped to one knee in front of her, and the cold of the tile seeped through his denim jeans. Absently he told himself to have a carpet installed. He didn't want Casey getting sick—or worse, slipping and falling on wet tile.

He took the plastic stick from her hand and barely glanced at the deep-pink test square. Instead, he folded his hands around hers and felt a twinge of guilt at the icy feel of her skin.

"I'm not sorry, Jake," she said softly. "I know you don't want this baby, but I do. And I'll love it enough for both of us."

"You're wrong, Casey."

She blinked at him, clearly surprised. He couldn't really blame her—he felt a little stunned himself. But he would get over it. The important thing to remember here was that baby hadn't made itself. And whatever else happened between him and Casey, his child wasn't going to suffer for it.

"It's *our* baby," he said firmly, willing her to believe him. "*We're* going to have a baby. In fact, this is the best Christmas present I've ever received." He moved and sat down beside her on the edge of the tub. Draping one arm around her shoulders, he pulled her against him. "Whatever this marriage started out like, we just became a family."

Eight

A baby.

Three weeks ago he'd been blissfully contentedly single. Now he was an expectant father and married to a woman he hadn't seen in years. Jake's gaze lifted heavenward. Somebody up there had a very interesting sense of humor.

Casey straightened and shook her head, still staring at the test stick as if she couldn't quite believe this was happening.

"You know, staring at it won't make it change color."

She swung her gaze to him. "This is so weird."

"Being pregnant?"

"Not just that." She paused. "Although that is definitely the weirdest part. It's this whole situation, Jake."

He let his arm slip from her shoulder as he scooted closer to her on the tub's edge.

"Three weeks ago everything was different," she said.

Jake scowled, despite the fact that he'd been thinking the same thing only a minute ago.

"I was supposed to marry Steven, for heaven's sake." Casey let her gaze drop back down to the stick she held.

Fortunately she didn't see him flinch at her words. It still rankled him that she'd been able to switch gears so quickly when it came to choosing husbands.

"But then," she went on, more to herself than to him, "if I *had* married Steven, none of this would be happening."

True enough, but hardly relevant. She hadn't married Steven. Everything *had* happened, and they'd damn well better start dealing with it.

She rubbed the tip of one finger across the dark pink test square. "I don't think Steven wanted children."

That caught his attention. "Don't you *know?*"

Casey shook her head. "We didn't really talk much." She shot him a quick look. "I guess that makes me sound even worse, doesn't it? I mean that I was willing to marry a man I didn't even talk to."

"Hell, Casey, I don't know." And he didn't. She

didn't strike him as the type of woman to be so cavalier with her affections. But then, what did he know about women? He'd married Linda.

"I don't even know how our engagement happened."

"What?"

"It's true. Sometimes I try to remember exactly when Steven proposed…"

It bothered him more than he wanted to admit that she'd been thinking about her ex-fiancé while married to *him*.

"But I don't think he ever really did. We both just drifted into this. Our parents were all for it, naturally."

Jake hadn't been too fond of Steven to begin with. Knowing that Casey's parents approved of the man made him even more disagreeable to Jake.

Abruptly deciding he'd heard quite enough about the runaway bridegroom, he pushed himself up from the edge of the tub and held one hand out to his wife.

"Enough about Steven, Casey."

She looked up at him, but didn't take the hand he offered.

"*We're* married now. *We* have a baby on the way."

"There's definitely a baby coming, Jake," she countered. "But as for being married, all we shared was a short ceremony."

"What?" Feeling a little foolish about his extended

hand, which she refused to take, Jake let it fall to his side. "What are you talking about?"

She stood up and faced him. Granted, she had to tip her head back to do it, but somehow she managed to look intimidating, anyway.

"I'm talking about us. You. Me."

"You're not making sense."

"No, this marriage doesn't make sense."

He inhaled slowly, deeply. He'd been working diligently for the past two weeks. He'd kept his distance. He'd lain awake at night knowing she was lying in a bed only a few doors down the hall from him. He'd become accustomed to walking with his legs slightly bowed to accommodate a groin that was continually hard and aching.

And he'd suffered all of it for her sake. Didn't she understand what it cost him to keep his distance from her? Couldn't she tell how little sleep he was getting by the shadows under his eyes? Should he tell her how he lay awake at nights thinking about her? Remembering the feel, the scent, the taste of her?

"If we're married," she went on, oblivious to the tightening of his features, "don't you think we should at least *pretend* to be a real couple?"

"We don't have to pretend. We *are* a real couple. Harry married us. You were there."

"We're not a couple, Jake. We're two people living in the same house. We're housemates."

He rubbed one hand across his face and struggled to draw air into his lungs. "Casey, I told you, I think we both need time to adjust to this."

"If you regret marrying me, Jake," she said calmly, "just say so. I'll have my father arrange a divorce. There's nothing he'd like better."

His gaze snapped to hers. Anger bubbled up inside him. He didn't care if it was reasonable or not. That she could talk so easily about a divorce bothered him more than he could say.

"There's no divorce coming, Casey." He gritted his teeth and went on, squeezing his voice past a tight throat. "Get used to it. I'm not going through that again. And dammit, I'm not going to let *my* child go through it."

Casey felt a chill from his words and expression, as she would have from a brisk northern wind. His eyes narrowed and she sensed the tension in him. She hadn't *meant* it. She didn't want a divorce. She wanted a husband. The husband she loved.

Apparently, though, she was going about it in all the wrong ways. Fine. Swallowing back her impatience, she said, "You're right. There is no divorce for us, Jake. I don't want that, either."

He seemed to relax a little, so she plunged ahead.

"But I want more than a housemate, too." She waited for him to argue with her. But he didn't say anything, so she went on, "I want someone to talk to. To laugh with. To plan with."

He was softening. She could see it in his eyes.

"To love," she added, and almost groaned as she saw tension arc back into his body.

"Let's leave love out of this, all right?"

"How do you leave love out of a marriage?"

He gave her a wry smile. "Trust me. It's easier to leave it out than to try to keep it in."

Disappointment quivered through her. Jake always had been stubborn. A less stubborn man would have given in to her clumsy seduction attempt five years before and saved both of them from missed chances at happiness. Casey frowned at him, studying the sharp planes of his face as she would a text written in an unfamiliar language.

Because of his sense of honor, his conscience, they had both lost the past five years. Casey had no doubt that if he hadn't turned her away that long-ago night, they would have known the magic that sparked between them for what it was. They would have stayed together. And maybe this child that was coming now would have been their second. Or third.

"Now come on," he said, and snatched up her hand. "Let's get you something to eat."

As they moved through the dark house headed for the kitchen, Jake turned on the lights they passed. Soon the big ranch house was well lit, warm and welcoming.

It struck her then exactly how she would have to go about winning her husband. One light at a time, until finally all the shadows were chased from his soul.

"See?" Jake straightened the aerial map lying on his desk and pointed to a section of land that had been highlighted in bright red ink.

Casey leaned over his shoulder, and he forced himself to take slow shallow breaths. Just the scent of her was enough to drive him insane. Having the length of her soft shining hair streaming alongside his cheek was especially dangerous. He knew what her hair smelled like. Roses and promises. If he took a deep breath, dragging that scent into him, there was no way he would be able to keep a grip on his rising tide of desire.

"Who drew the red line around it?" she asked, and tilted her head to look at him.

"Me." Deliberately he shifted his gaze from hers. Staring into emerald green eyes was not the way to maintain an even keel. "I've wanted that land for years. Outlined it to help me focus on it."

"Ah."

The knowing tone in her voice made him turn to look at her again, despite his better judgment. For the past few days, ever since the night they'd discovered her pregnancy, he'd made a concerted effort to be a better husband. These days, after dinner, they sat together in the great room. They watched movies, idiotic television shows that he couldn't concentrate on with her sitting beside him, and they talked about his plans for the ranch or the catering jobs she'd been offered. He listened to her talk excitedly of their first Christmas together and tried to share her eagerness.

They did everything together but share a bedroom. It didn't matter that all he thought about these days was being with her. Holding her. Sliding into her warmth and burying himself inside her. Danger lay down that path. That was a risk he still couldn't bring himself to take. Not yet.

But there was something else to consider, too. He had no intention of being celibate for the rest of his life. So what he had to do was give himself enough time to distance himself emotionally from Casey before starting in on the physical side of their marriage. Once he'd accomplished that, everything would go much more smoothly.

She was watching him.

He pushed his thoughts aside and reached back to pick up the threads of their conversation.

"What do you mean, ah?"

"Nothing." She lifted one shoulder in an elegant shrug. "It's just that I had no idea you were interested in positive visualization."

"Positive what?"

"Visualization." Casey straightened and took a step to one side. Jake drew his first easy breath since they'd entered his office.

"I don't know what you're talking about," he said. "All I did was draw a line around something I wanted."

"Exactly. Positive visualization means that you focus your energies on the object of your desire and harness the energies of the universe to help you get it."

He laughed. He couldn't help it. She looked so damned serious. As if telling the universe was all you needed to do to solve your problems. Shaking his head, he felt his laughter slowly drain away as he noticed she wasn't laughing with him.

"Several books have been written on the subject, you know."

"Books have been written on UFOs, too."

Her lips twitched. "Hardly the same thing."

"Right." He nodded sagely. "Different universes."

"Although," Casey said thoughtfully, "those books

are very interesting. I believe my favorite is the one about gods in chariots."

Jake snorted and rolled his eyes.

"Fine," she said as she turned for the door. "All I'm saying is that you focused your energies and the universe's, and you got what you wanted."

"Sure," Jake countered, getting to his feet and following her. "As soon as I came up with the cash Don wanted for the land."

"Exactly."

He laughed again. Odd, but he didn't remember laughing so much in years as he had the past few days with Casey. "What's *that* mean?"

She settled onto her end of the long couch in the main room and waited for him to sit down beside her before answering. "You were able to find the money once the universe had obliged you by arranging everything else."

Jake leaned his head back against the cushions and stared up at the ceiling. "You're amazing."

"Thank you."

He wasn't prepared. He hadn't heard a thing. When at least thirty pounds of snuffling drooling fur landed on his stomach, his breath whooshed out of him.

"Hello, baby," Casey crooned, and laughed as the dog wriggled ecstatically on Jake's stomach.

"Get off, you flea-bitten mangy excuse for a dog!"

The big puppy's head drooped and both ears flopped down to rest against its cheeks.

"Jake, you hurt his feelings."

If the dog had landed an inch or two lower on his abdomen, it would have hurt something a tad more precious to Jake than his feelings. Looking into sad brown eyes, though, he did feel almost guilty for shouting.

Almost.

"It's all right, Stumbles," Casey soothed. "Come over here, and never mind Daddy."

Jake's eyes widened. "I am *not* that dog's daddy."

She wasn't paying any attention to him. But then, neither was the dog. For a moment he watched as his wife cuddled and stroked the ugliest animal he'd ever seen.

Gray and black hair stood out in odd tufts over its forehead and legs. Its ears were lopsided, giving the impression that the dog's head was continually cocked, and it had the biggest feet Jake had ever seen on anything smaller than an elephant. He shuddered to even think about how big that hound was going to get.

He still wasn't sure exactly how they'd come to own a dog. He wasn't entirely certain that Casey knew, either. Stumbles, so christened because he tripped over his own feet, had simply appeared one evening at dinnertime and hadn't left.

Yet.

Casey had immediately dubbed the puppy their "Christmas visitor" and calmly informed Jake that it would bring terrible luck down on them if they were to turn him away.

"He's not ugly," she said quietly.

Jake's gaze shot to hers. "How'd you know that's what I was thinking?"

"It wasn't hard. You say it often enough." Stumbles scooted himself around until he lay in the small space separating Casey and Jake on the couch. Laying his head on his mistress's thigh, he closed his eyes and promptly began to snore.

Jake's eyebrows lifted as he took in the animal's position. A hell of a note—envying a disreputable hound.

"I always wanted a dog," she whispered.

Jake watched her fingertips trace lightly over Stumbles's ragged fur. Her voice sounded so wistful his insides twisted, bringing a pain he didn't want to feel. Or acknowledge. He could just imagine what her parents' reaction to a dog like Stumbles would have been. They would have called the pound immediately of course. And no one visiting the shelter to adopt a cute puppy would have given Stumbles a glance.

Jake frowned and looked at the happily snoring mutt. If not for Casey, Stumbles would no doubt have ended up walking that long last mile.

Instantly memories of Casey as a teenager raced through his mind. He recalled how much she'd loved the animals on the ranch. From the barn cats to the horses, she'd never been able to get enough. No doubt, the Oakeses' idea of a family pet was the buffalo on one side of a nickel.

It must have been hard for someone as loving and caring as Casey to grow up in such a cold home.

He pushed that notion aside and said gruffly, "Well, if he's going to stay, we'd better get him to the vet for his shots."

Casey grinned and Jake felt oddly rewarded.

"He'll need a collar, too," she said. "And tags. We wouldn't want anyone to steal him."

Jake laughed and Stumbles snorted, clearly disturbed by the racket. There wasn't a chance in hell that anyone but Casey would steal the ugly Stumbles. But if she wanted to get the dog collared and tagged, that was what they would do.

He was just being nice, he told himself. After all, she was the mother of his child.

It was the least he could do.

* * *

A few days later Casey stood in the modern well-equipped ranch kitchen and surveyed her handiwork. Every muscle in her body ached. She'd been up half the night completing this order, but it was worth it.

So many things had changed in such a short amount of time. Married, pregnant and, apparently, a new and flourishing career.

"Who would have thought it, Stumbles?" she murmured to the dog lying beneath the kitchen table.

His tail thumped against the floor and a low pleading whine issued from his throat.

"Not a chance," she said on a laugh. "These goodies are not for you."

Sorrowfully the dog laid his head down on his paws and watched her as she walked the length of the room, inspecting everything.

She looked at the carefully arranged trays laid out on the countertops and went over the list in her hand for the third time.

"Napoleons, check. Crème brûlées, check. Eclairs, check." Each and every order received a final inspection. "Ladyfingers, check. Petits fours, check. And cookies…" Dozens of them—stars, angels, santas—each dusted with crushed silver dragées and looking fit for a fairy feast. When she reached the end of the counter, she sighed and nodded to herself.

Finished. And if she did say so herself, a nice job, too.

This was by far the most important catering job she'd been offered since the wedding. The Ladies Guild of Greater Simpson's annual Christmas fund-raiser could be the start of something wonderful for her. Or, a little voice inside taunted, a fiery crash into disaster.

"Ready?"

She spun around to see Jake, standing in the doorway. Dressed in jeans, a worn flannel shirt, with the sleeves rolled up past his elbows, he took her breath away. He leaned against the doorjamb, arms folded over his chest, his blue eyes fixed on her in a way that made her heart race and her mouth go dry.

Yet even as she watched him, that look faded from his eyes and was replaced by a detached friendly concern. Casey felt a familiar swell of disappointment rise in her. It didn't seem to matter that they were getting along better and better. It didn't seem to count with him that they had fun together. They still weren't sharing a bedroom. He still insisted on holding himself back from her. Not just his body.

His heart.

"Casey?"

"Hmm?" She shook her head. "Sorry. Daydreaming, I guess."

He nodded and pushed away from the doorway. Walking toward her, he said, "So, are you ready to go?"

"Jake, you don't have to take me to town. I can drive the truck myself."

"No trouble. Besides, I don't want you lifting all these trays in and out of the truck bed."

She inhaled deeply and nodded.

"You look tired," he said, and his husky voice sent awareness skittering through her.

She swallowed back her reaction and said, "I am. The order took most of the night."

"It's not good for you," he told her, "staying up that late. Working this hard." His gaze swept over her quickly, thoroughly. "You're pregnant, Casey. You need to get rest."

"I'm fine, Jake."

He didn't look convinced.

"When's your doctor's appointment?"

"This afternoon. At three."

"You sure the doctor won't mind if I'm there, too, will she?"

She smiled at him. "She said that all fathers are welcome—as long as they behave."

"Good." He nodded and picked up the flattened pastry boxes. As he folded one of them into shape, he said, "I want to ask her about all this catering stuff you're doing. Don't want you injuring yourself or the baby."

"Jake…"

"It won't hurt to ask."

She sighed and changed the subject. "I thought I'd visit with Annie until it was time to go to the doctor's office."

"OK," he said, then picked up a tray of éclairs and slid it into the waiting box. "I've got some business in town, so we can deliver your goodies first, then drop you off at the hairdresser. I'll pick you up when it's time."

She knew it would be pointless to argue. She'd tried to tell him there was no need for him to accompany her to the doctor. He hadn't listened then, so there was no reason to suppose he would listen now.

Whatever else she could say about him, he certainly seemed determined to be a good father.

That was a start.

Wasn't it?

Nine

"I think I'm losing my mind."

Frank Parrish laughed at his son's serious tone and waved him to a chair. "You're not losing your mind, Jake. You're just spending too much time arguing with your common sense, instead of listening to it."

Jake turned away from the window and the view of Simpson City Park. Several men were setting up the town Christmas tree. He was *not* in a holiday frame of mind. Studying his father, seated in a worn but comfortable easy chair, he asked, "What's that supposed to mean?"

"I think you know what it means, and that's what's got you so scared."

"Scared?" He barked a laugh and shook his head. "I'm certainly not scared, Dad."

"Don't know what else you'd call it, then," Frank said. "You've got a real nice wife—pretty, too. A baby on the way, a good ranch, big house and all the land you've ever wanted. If you're not scared, why aren't you happy?"

It did sound ridiculous when put like that. But dammit, he'd had most of those things before, too. And it hadn't changed anything. Linda had still walked out. Leaving him reeling.

How could he risk having Casey do the same thing?

"She's not Linda," his father said softly.

"I never said she was."

"You didn't have to say it. It's in your eyes every day."

"What?"

"Every day, you're waiting for the ax to fall. You keep looking out for the thunderclouds, you never notice the sunshine."

"And if I'm not watching for the storm, I get caught up in it. Then what?"

"You get wet."

Jake laughed shortly.

"Then you dry off again and start over."

"No, thanks." If the storm came this time, Jake knew it would be far worse than the drizzle he had faced at Linda's hands. He was sure of it, because he cared far more for Casey than he had ever thought possible.

Every day spent with her was a good day. Listening to her, hearing her move around the once-silent house with that damned dog at her heels, was like music to him. He hadn't even known how lonely he really was until Casey had come.

But if he let himself care for her, if he told her he loved her, only to lose her, the pain would kill him.

"It's your decision of course."

"What is?" Jake's gaze locked with his father's.

"To let yourself enjoy the second chance you've been given."

Jake stiffened and shook his head.

"Or," Frank went on, "to turn your back on it and live the half life you've been living for the past few years."

Some choice.

Lonely?

Or dead inside because he took a chance?

"So, how you feeling these days, pregnant lady?"

Casey grinned at Annie. "Great." The grin slipped a bit. "Aren't I supposed to be feeling terrible? Do you think something's wrong?"

"I think everything's fine and you worry too much." Annie pulled a wide-toothed comb through her customer's wet iron gray hair. "You should be like Mrs. Dieter here. Don't worry about a thing." She raised her voice to a near shout. "Isn't that right, Mrs. Dieter?"

"Who's gonna fight?" the old lady yelled.

Casey laughed quietly, briefly met Annie's amused gaze, then looked around. The sharp distinctive odor of permanent solution hung in the air of the tiny beauty shop. Annie was the owner and sole employee, so her customers always had to wait, but as Annie liked to tell them, she was worth it.

Casey wandered around the small room, admiring pots of flowers and hanging plants that made the waiting area look like a rain forest. Gold and silver stars were sprinkled amid the greenery, and life-size posters of both Santa Claus and Frosty the Snowman were hung on the walls. Multicolored lights twinkled around the windowframe, and Christmas carols drifted quietly from a tape player in the corner.

A floor-to-ceiling bookshelf along one wall was lined with paperbacks, and the latest magazines and mail-order catalogs lay scattered across a low table set in the middle of four overstuffed chairs.

Since she was waiting to go to lunch with Annie,

Casey sat down in one of those chairs, snatched up a catalog and made herself comfortable.

"I won't be much longer," Annie said. "Mrs. Dieter was an emergency cut. Her grandson's coming to take her out on the town." Annie's voice rose in volume again. "Joe's quite the dancer."

"How can I answer you if I can't hear your question?" The old lady sniffed and closed her eyes, apparently deciding to catch a quick nap in the chair.

With a smile Annie glanced at Casey and asked, "So how's my big brother taking the news of impending fatherhood?"

"I think he's pleased about the whole thing." Actually she wasn't sure, but she certainly heard Jake muttering, "A *baby*," to himself often enough to know he was thinking about it.

"Well, why shouldn't he be?"

Indeed. Casey only wished he was half as pleased about being a husband. Oh, things had definitely improved between them in the short time since she'd done the pregnancy test. They actually *talked* in the evenings. Jake was always solicitous, offering to make her tea, bring her a pillow. He was sort of the 1950s movie version of a soon-to-be father. The only thing he hadn't done was boil water.

But they still slept in separate rooms, and any time

the conversation took a turn to the personal, he took a turn to the door. Emotionally speaking of course.

"How's everything…else going?"

Casey glanced up from the catalog. "The same," she said, and hated the defeated note in her voice. But really, what more could she do? She'd tried seducing him five years before. Apparently she wasn't very good at it.

Besides, how did you go about seducing your husband?

"Jake always was too stubborn for his own good. It's amazing you even *got* pregnant." Annie tugged at a stubborn knot, and the old woman opened her eyes to glare at her in the mirror. "Sorry, Mrs. Dieter."

Casey folded the corner of a page down over a couple of items she wanted to order, then asked, "You think one of these magazines of yours will have an article on how to get your husband back in bed?"

Annie opened her mouth, but Mrs. Dieter cut her off.

"Meet him at the door naked," she said sharply. "Worked on Mr. Dieter every time."

Casey looked at Annie.

Annie looked at Casey.

Then they both stared at the wizened old woman.

"For Christmas," Mrs. Dieter added, "I used to wear a big ol' red ribbon tied around my chest with a great big bow right in the middle of my boobies." She glanced down sadly at her pendulous breasts. "I had real perky boobies back then, too. Always brightened Mr. Dieter right up, seeing them."

A stunned silence stretched out in the room before the woman snapped, "You think I was *born* old?"

Annie laughed first, then bent down and kissed the woman's papery cheek. "Mrs. Dieter, today's hairstyle is on the house."

"You may call me Agnes."

As Annie and Agnes laughed together, Casey sank back into the cushions. Staring blankly out the window, she giggled and told herself that what was good for Mr. Dieter, might just be good for Mr. Parrish.

On the way from the snowy parking lot to the doctor's office, Casey and Jake passed four people who stopped to offer congratulations on their coming baby. As the last well-wisher moved off, Casey said, "Now how do you suppose everybody found out about the baby already?"

Jake took her hand and pulled her toward the shiny new medical building. "No supposing about it," he said wryly. "I told you that Emma with a phone in her hand could outdo supermarket tabloids."

"She's *good*," Casey muttered.

He glanced down at her and smiled. "Now aren't

you glad we only told her and Uncle Harry yesterday? Think what she could have done if she'd had more than a week."

"It chills the blood." Casey shook her head and hurried to keep pace with Jake's long strides. Emma and Harry weren't the only people they'd waited to tell. She still had to break the news to her parents that they were going to have a grandchild. Talk about blood-chilling.

A few minutes later they were being ushered through the empty waiting room to the examining room. Casey stepped behind a dressing screen, took off her clothes and donned a ridiculously sheer open-in-the-back, pink cotton gown. When she climbed onto the table, she turned to Jake.

"You don't have to stay for this part, you know. You could just come in when the doctor's finished and ask any questions you might have."

He glanced at the cold steel stirrups, already up and waiting for her feet, then shifted his gaze back to her. "It's all right. If you don't mind, I'd rather stay."

She squeezed a laugh past her suddenly tight throat. "It's OK with me."

A moment later Dr. Dianna Hauck bustled into the room, her nurse right behind her, and grinned at them.

"So," the doctor began, "pregnant, huh?"

"That's what the test kit says."

The doctor shook her head and said wryly, "Those blasted kits are putting me out of business." Glancing at Jake, she asked, "You staying?"

"If it's all right."

"OK by me, just keep out of the way." Dr. Hauck laughed, pulled up a stool and sank onto it. "That's what I'll be telling you when we're in the delivery room, so get used to it."

Jake inhaled sharply and one of the doctor's eyebrows lifted.

"OK, Casey, take the position." The nurse handed Dr. Hauck a pair of latex gloves and she snapped them on.

Jake took the woman at her word and moved to the head of the table. Casey reached back and took his hand. His fingers curled around hers. Her skin felt cold. Was she as nervous as he was?

What if the kit had been wrong? What if there was no baby? Would he be pleased? Or disappointed? He looked down into Casey's green eyes and saw his own anxieties staring back at him.

It was over in a matter of minutes.

"You can sit up now," the doctor said as she rose and walked to the sink, pulling off her gloves as she went. While she washed her hands, she looked over her shoulder at them. "My best guess is that in about eight months or so you'll be parents."

Jake released a breath he hadn't realized he'd been holding. A warm delightful feeling settled in his chest. That settled that. He was pleased about the baby.

Moving closer to Casey, he instinctively tightened his grip on her hand and began asking all of the usual about-to-be-a-father questions.

The very next evening Casey turned the dimmer on the kitchen light switch until the room was softly lit. She raised the lid on the pot at the back of the stove, gave the contents a quick stir, then resettled the lid.

She looked around the room. Stumbles wasn't around, tucked into his blanket in Jake's office. The table was elegantly set. Counters and cooking island cleaned off. Fire burning in the hearth. Beef stew simmering. Freshly made éclairs waiting in the refrigerator.

Everything was ready.

Even her.

She smoothed her hair one last time as she heard Jake's Jeep pull into the yard. Tossing a quick glance out the curtained window, she saw him climb out of the Jeep and reach back inside for the tools he'd picked up at the hardware store.

Her stomach flipped over and she took a deep steadying breath. It was time to find out if Mrs. Dieter knew what she was talking about.

She glanced down at herself, sighed, then tugged at the wide red ribbon tied around her chest. The bow between her breasts was a little crooked, but she didn't think Jake would mind. She hoped he would be too busy doing something else to worry about the aesthetics.

She shivered in the somewhat cool room and told herself she should have stayed closer to the fireplace. Naked but for the bright red bow, she was beginning to get downright cold. Not to mention just a tad uneasy.

Inhaling sharply, she tried not to think about what she might be setting herself up for. She groaned quietly at the humiliating images leaping to life in her mind. What if he walked in the door, took one look at her and *laughed?* Or worse yet, walked right past her and didn't even *notice* she was naked?

Won't happen, she told herself. She knew darn well he wanted her every bit as much as she did him.

The outside door opened, then shut again, and Casey tensed. If this little stunt didn't reach him, she wasn't sure what would. She struck a pose, hoping to look nonchalant, and waited.

Jake set the bag down on a table, then stopped in the mudroom long enough to shrug out of his coat, tug off his boots and toss them onto the newspaper spread out alongside the door. He sniffed the air, appreciating the delicious aroma drifting from the kitchen. A man could get used to this. It wasn't so long ago that he had come home from a long day to an empty house and a frozen microwave dinner.

But that was before Casey.

He slumped back against the wall and asked himself how he was going to keep living with his wife and not make love to her. It was harder every day to ignore her presence. To ignore the small but pleasant changes she'd made to the house. To his life.

How could he live with her and *not* fall in love with her?

Keep remembering Linda, he thought. Remember what it had been like to find out she'd been lying about loving him. Remember the pain.

Nodding abruptly, he straightened and crossed to the sink on the opposite wall. He washed up quickly, then moved to the kitchen door. He stepped into the warm fragrant room and all rational thought dissolved.

"Merry Christmas, Jake."

He blinked, shook his head and blinked again as if expecting the apparition in front of him to disappear.

"Casey?"

His body tightened as his gaze swept over her. In the soft light her skin looked as pale and creamy as fine porcelain. The wide ribbon wrapped around her chest and across her erect nipples came together in a slightly askew bow in the valley between her breasts. The ends of the ribbon trailed across her abdomen, drawing his gaze down to the light brown triangle of curls at the juncture of her thighs. As he admired her, she shifted position and the ribbon swayed gently with her movement.

Mouth dry, heart pounding in his chest, Jake knew his valiant struggle was over. No more battling his instincts. No more distance between them. At some point he would have to find a way to live with this incredible—and surprising—woman without falling in love with her.

But not today.

"It's three weeks until Christmas," he said finally, and congratulated himself on getting his voice to work.

"Close enough." She shrugged and his breath caught as the ribbon across her breasts dipped a bit.

His gaze stroked across her body, slowly, hungrily. A Christmas package. Santa had never been *this* good to him before.

Minutes ticked by. He had to say something. But what?

"Dinner smells good." Brilliant.

"Beef stew."

He nodded and noticed the grip she had on the edge of the cooking island. Her knuckles were white.

Nerves? Swinging his gaze back to hers, he asked, "What's for dessert?"

She cleared her throat, again shifted from foot to foot and glanced at the refrigerator. "Chocolate éclairs."

"I'd rather have you."

Her breath caught, the tension in her shoulders eased, and she released her death grip on the island. She took a hesitant step toward him and Jake wanted to kick himself. Had he done this to her? Made her so anxious? So unsure of herself? Yes, he had.

To protect himself. Something to be proud of, he thought with disgust. Whether they had planned this marriage or not, Casey was his *wife* and deserved better than she had gotten so far from him.

Starting now, this minute, he would give her everything he could give. And hopefully it would be enough to keep her from missing what he simply didn't have anymore.

"Jake?"

He smiled and watched the lines between her finely arched brows disappear. "I don't believe I've ever been welcomed home so warmly."

"Welcome? Yes," she said, and grinned wryly. "Warm?" She shivered a bit. "Not really."

Goose bumps raced along her arms and legs. He went to her quickly and pulled her into his arms.

Running his hands up and down her supple body, he whispered, "Maybe you should have waited to try this in the summer."

"I didn't want to wait," she said, and drew her head back to look at him. "Not anymore."

He lifted one hand to caress her cheek and groaned when she turned a kiss into his palm. "I'm glad you didn't wait."

"Me, too."

Glancing down at her ribbon-wrapped body, he gave her a half smile before asking, "Am I allowed to open my Christmas present this early?"

"You're allowed just about anything tonight," she said softly. She trembled again and his right hand began to stroke up and down her spine.

"Still cold?" he whispered.

Another tremor rocketed through her. "Not now."

"Good," he said just before he dipped his head to claim the kiss for which, he'd been hungering for days.

She leaned into him, liquid sensual heat, and Jake knew the moment his mouth came down on hers that no matter what else happened between them, he would never again keep himself from her. As long as she wanted him, he would be there.

Her lips parted his and his tongue thrust inside to restake his claim on her. Caressing, exploring, he rediscovered her with all of the eagerness and excitement of their first night together.

He felt her hands slide up his arms to his shoulders. Felt her fingers spear through his hair. Her breath puffed against his cheek. His hands moved up and down her back in long smooth motions over skin that seemed as perfect, as sleek as the finest china.

Raising one hand, he cupped her breast and, through the satiny texture of the ribbon, rubbed his thumb across her hardened nipple until a low deep-throated moan escaped her. She arched against him and Jake held her tighter, closer.

Her hands slipped to the front of his shirt and beneath the soft flannel fabric to his chest. He shuddered at her touch, then pulled back from her only long enough to tug his shirt off and toss it to the floor.

She reached for him, but he caught her hands. His gaze moved over her slowly, admiringly. "When someone gives me a package, all neatly done up in ribbon, it's *my* present. Right?"

"Yeah…"

"And," he said as he reached for one dangling end of the ribbon, "you *did* say I was allowed *anything* tonight, didn't you?"

"Yeah, I guess so." She shivered a bit as he tugged on the ribbon.

The big bow came loose and fell to the floor at her feet in a whisper of sound. Jake smiled and both black eyebrows rose as he set his hands at her waist and lifted her to sit on the edge of the cooking island.

"What are you up to?" she asked.

"Why, Casey," he admonished, and took the few steps to the refrigerator, "don't you trust me?"

"Sure, but what…" Her voice faded as she watched him pull the chocolate éclairs out of the fridge.

He set the tray of pastries on the table, then picked up one éclair and walked back to her. Dipping his index finger into the luscious cream filling, he scooped out a generous dollop, held it toward her and said softly, "I'm having my dessert first."

Ten

The countertop under her bottom was cold, but the look in Jake's eyes made the blood in her veins sizzle.

She swallowed heavily and watched him come closer. When her knees brushed his bare chest, he stopped. Seated on the cooking island, she was at eye level with her husband, and she kept her gaze locked with his as he offered her the fingerful of heavy sweetened cream. The flavor exploded in her mouth, but when she reached for the éclair to offer some to him, Jake shook his head.

"I'll get my own," he said softly, then bent to taste first one of her breasts, then the other. Tenderly, delicately, his tongue stroked her nipples as if she were indeed a rare luscious dessert. Her fingers curled around the edge of the island and she held on tight as wave after wave of delight crashed through her.

Sharp dagger points of need began to stab at her center, making her ache with wanting him. A deep inner throbbing pulsed along with her heartbeat, and her breath came in ragged gasps. Arching into his wonderful mouth, she offered herself to him, hoping for, needing, more.

He chuckled gently and lifted his head. "*My* present," he reminded her with one quick kiss on her lips.

Ridiculous to suddenly feel...not *uneasy. Embarrassed?* This whole naked-in-the-kitchen thing had seemed like such a good idea at the time. She noted the gleam in his eye and experienced an answering tremor that shook her insides. The brief attack of awkwardness disappeared in a rush of something she could only describe as...intoxicating.

"Jake," she said, her voice just a touch playful, "nice men don't torture their wives."

"Ah," he countered with a wink, "but what wife wants her husband to be *nice?*"

"Me?"

"No, you don't, Casey," he assured her, and eased her back until she was lying down on the island, knees bent at the edge and her feet dangling. "You much prefer me *adventurous*."

"Just how adventurous are we talking about here?" Nerves fluttered in her chest again. "Maybe I should warn you that I'm not normally the adventurous type."

"That's not what your ribbon said."

True. No way to argue that. But then, she admitted silently, she didn't really want to argue with whatever he had in mind. She'd waited long enough for this moment and damned if she wouldn't enjoy herself.

She lifted her head to watch him as he walked to the end of the island and positioned himself between her legs. She gasped when he dipped one finger into the éclair filling again and reached for her.

"Jake..."

"My present," he reminded her. "My dessert."

Then he touched the icy filling to her hottest flesh, and she jumped, startled at the sensation. "It's cold!"

"Not for long," he said, and his voice sounded thick, husky.

Casey shuddered. Through half-closed eyes, she watched him as he lowered his mouth to her center. As he covered her, she groaned and let her head drop back to the countertop.

His tongue smoothed through the cool thick cream, swirling it around her flesh, stroking it, tasting it. He lapped at her body with a slow deliberation that pushed Casey's nerve endings into a frenzy of need. Her legs parted farther, inviting him closer, deeper.

He drove her toward madness and taunted her with release. His mouth created fires of desperation, and his tongue introduced her to delights she hadn't dreamed existed.

With every intimate caress, he became more a part of her. He touched more than her body. He touched her heart. Her soul.

As much as her body hummed from his attentions, her soul soared. This is what they were meant to be, she thought dazedly. His touch reached beyond the physical and eased her spirit.

Together.

Forever.

"Jake…" She felt it coming. Her body tightened in expectation. Tingles of awareness brightened, glowing inside her like a Fourth of July fireworks display. Her breath caught. She reached for the prize dangling just out of her grasp. She strained, aching for the completion he offered her. Then a spectacular bolt of pure pleasure rocketed through her. She stiffened and cried his name in a strangled voice.

A few moments later she lay limp on the counter and felt him delicately washing away the last of the sugared cream filling from her body. She jumped as he brushed over the still-sensitive flesh. When he finally finished, she opened her eyes to look up at him.

Passion darkened his gaze, and though her climax had only just passed, she felt desperate for him again. To feel him atop her. Inside her. Joined to her as deeply as he had been on that magical night that had led to their marriage. She reached for him and cuddled close to his chest as he scooped her up and carried her down the hallway to the master bedroom.

He laid her in the center of the mattress, tore off the rest of his clothes and lay down beside her. His hands moved over her roughly, hurriedly, as if he had waited too long to touch her. As if he couldn't touch her enough.

Desperation rose in Jake and shattered inside his chest. Need like he'd never known before swamped him. His body ached for her. Casey's flesh beneath his hands became a song in his brain that repeated over and over. A tune he couldn't name and couldn't forget. A melody that had somehow, despite his efforts to prevent it, etched its way into his heart and become as much a part of his life as breathing.

She kissed him, opening her mouth to him, inviting his caress. She took his breath for her own and gave him hers. And when he couldn't bear to be separate from her another moment, she opened her body to him, welcoming him inside.

He groaned aloud as he pushed into her and felt her heat surround him, invade him. She locked her legs around his hips and held him tight within her until his world finally exploded, leaving only her warmth to shelter him.

A short time later they lay entwined on the bed, Casey's head pillowed on his chest. Jake ran one hand up and down her back, marveling at the softness of her skin and the incredible gift of having her in his life.

Even as he thought it, though, he turned from the realization that he was coming to care too much for her. He wouldn't let it happen again. He wouldn't allow himself to be such a fool for love that when it was over he was left with nothing.

She stirred against him, dropped a quick kiss on his chest and draped one arm across his body.

It felt good. Right.

And terrifying.

"Is dinner ruined?" He blurted the question in self-defense, to keep himself from wandering too far down a path he couldn't risk taking.

"You can think about food at a time like this?" she teased, and raised herself on one elbow to look at him.

"I don't have the strength to think of anything else." He flicked her a glance and smiled tiredly. "Not until I get something to eat."

"Then by all means," she countered, "let's feed you."

She rolled to one side and snatched up one of his T-shirts from a stack of fresh laundry. Holding it up in front of her, she asked, "Shall we dress for dinner?"

Her short shapely legs peeked out from under the hem of the dark green shirt. She wiggled from side to side, giving him a tantalizing glimpse of her hips.

"Nice wives don't torture their husbands."

"As you'd already pointed out, I believe I prefer adventurous to nice."

His gaze narrowed. "Don't toy with a hungry man, woman. Toss me those sweats."

"The honeymoon's over." She sighed dramatically and tugged on his oversize T-shirt. Then she picked up his navy blue sweatpants and crawled back on the bed to deliver them personally. Dropping them on his stomach, she sat back on her heels and grinned at him. "I *do* love you, Jake Parrish."

The silence following that statement stretched out for what seemed hours.

What could he say that wouldn't make him sound like the bastard he knew he was? So he said nothing, taking the familiar route of hiding from something that cut too close to home. Sitting up, he pulled the sweatpants on, then stood and walked to his dresser for a shirt. Anything to keep from gazing into her eyes and what was surely a stricken look.

"I guess the honeymoon really *is* over," she said finally, and scooted to the edge of the bed.

Jake inhaled deeply, shoved his arms into the sleeves of a plain white T-shirt, then pulled it on. When he had no other choice, he turned to look at her.

"Casey—"

"Don't." She held up one hand toward him and shook her head.

"Don't what?"

"Don't tell me about how this is a different sort of marriage and love wasn't a part of the bargain."

"Well, was it?"

"For me, yes." She pushed herself off the bed and took a step toward the door. Then she stopped and looked at him again. Jake felt her gaze slice into him and knew he deserved it. "Fine. You don't—or *won't*—love me."

"It's not you," he argued. He didn't want to hurt her, so he gave her as much of the truth as he was able. "It's me. I don't think I'm capable of love anymore."

"That's bull, Jake."

"What?" Surprised, he stared at her and even from

across the room, saw the flash of anger that glittered in her eyes.

"You heard me."

"Casey—"

"No. What we just experienced together was—"

"Lust," he finished for her. "Pure and simple."

"Is that all you felt? Really?"

His gaze dropped a fraction and Casey saw it. She knew he had felt a hell of a lot more than lust. It was in his touch. In his kiss. In his every embrace. He loved her. But he was too damned stubborn to admit it.

"There's no reason we can't be happy in this marriage, Casey. We can be husband and wife. Enjoy each other. Raise our children and have as good a marriage, if not better, than most people have."

She nodded and waited for him to finish.

He took a deep breath and said, "Don't ask for what I can't give you, Casey. It will only hurt both of us."

Amazing. Did he actually *believe* that garbage?

Facing him, she crossed her arms over her chest and tilted her head to one side to stare at him.

"You're wrong, Jake."

He blinked and defensively folded his own arms across his chest.

"You don't want me to expect love from you? All right, I won't. But that's *your* loss, Jake. Not mine."

He lifted his chin as if expecting a blow, and she delivered it with her next words.

"I *do* love you, you big idiot. But as of right now, I'm through saying it."

"What's that supposed to mean?"

"It means that you can go ahead and pretend anything you like. But you *love* me, Jake Parrish. I know it." She crossed the room to him in several angry strides, not stopping until she was directly in front of him.

Poking his chest with her index finger to underline each word, she went on, "We'll be husband and wife. We'll enjoy each other. Raise our children. But until you can admit that you love me, we'll have only *half* a marriage."

"Casey—"

"And you'll have to be the first one to say it, Jake. I won't tell you again that I love you. Not until you've said it to me."

He shook his head slightly, and she wanted to kick him.

"You will say it, Jake. You will, or you'll be cheating yourself—and *me* out of something precious few people ever feel."

He reached for her, but she jumped back.

"Casey, can't you see that I'm only trying to protect both of us?"

"No. All I see is a man too hardheaded for his own good."

His jaw tightened and his gaze narrowed.

Casey nodded abruptly and turned her back on him. Headed for the doorway, she called over her shoulder, "Now come and have dinner, Jake. You'll need your strength."

"My strength," he repeated.

"Sure." She stopped, half turned and smiled at him. "I'm not going to cheat myself out of loving you or making love with you just because you're too stubborn to see what's right in front of you." Then she was gone, leaving him alone in the half-light.

"Casey…" She really was going to act as though nothing was wrong. She was going to go on and have a marriage whether he helped or not. He felt like an idiot.

He stared after her for a long moment and tried to figure out what had gone wrong with his perfectly reasonable plan.

A week later he was still trying.

One hairy lopsided ear slapped his cheek, and just to add insult to injury, Stumbles turned and barked in his face.

"All right," Jake muttered, pushing the dog off his

lap and onto the passenger seat. "Look out your own window for a while."

Obligingly Stumbles rose on his hind legs, curled his front paws over the lowered window glass and leaned his head out into the forty-mile-an-hour wind.

Jake scowled at the mutt, then swung his gaze back to stare blankly out the windshield. There had been no snow all week, and the sun had turned the earlier snowfalls into slushy mud. Everything was brown. Which matched his mood. He'd driven this same lonely stretch of road so many times he could have done it blindfolded. Even in the muck. Since no concentration was necessary, his mind began to wander. Naturally it wandered straight to Casey.

A whole week and she had been as good as her word. Not one more peep out of her about love and forever. They made love, spent their days and their evenings together. He helped her with her growing list of catering clients and gratefully accepted her assistance with the ranch books. They talked about the baby and Christmas, played with Stumbles and planned a nursery. Just yesterday they'd gone out and chopped down a tall Scotch pine and dragged it back to the house to be decorated. They ate together, slept together and did everything any other married couple did.

He grumbled, shifted in the seat and slammed his palm against the steering wheel.

Stumbles whined.

"Sorry," he said, then laughed at himself for apologizing to a dog.

Dammit, he was getting exactly what he'd insisted he'd wanted. Why wasn't he happy?

Because he missed hearing those three little words from her.

He missed seeing the words in her eyes.

"Hell." He glanced at the dog. "She even tells *you* she loves you."

Stumbles whined again, stretched out on the seat and laid his head on his master's thigh.

"Yeah, I know. I love you, too." Jake reached down and scratched behind the dog's ears. Stumbles scooted closer.

"Strange, don't you think? I can say those words to you. But not to her."

In the distance a large dark brown van pulled out of the ranch drive and started down the road toward Jake, obviously headed back to town.

He squinted into the afternoon sunshine and fought a growing tide of unease rising inside him. The closer he got to that damned van, the worse he felt. When they were separated by no more than ten feet, Jake pulled to one side and stopped to let the vehicle pass.

Long after the driver's friendly wave, he still sat there. Engine idling, dog climbing over him, he simply stared through the windshield at the house.

It had started again.

"Yes, I know, Mother," Casey was saying as he stomped into the kitchen. "I only thought you'd want to know. I never expected you to *do* anything."

He glanced at her. She smiled, but he didn't return it. He couldn't. Not now. Not when everything he'd feared would happen had only just begun.

"I'm sure Father is more than ready to go," Casey said, and rolled her eyes at Jake. "Yes, Paris is probably very pretty right now."

Paris.

Casey held up her index finger as if telling him she would only be another minute or two.

"Mother, I realize you're not the grandmother type. No one *expects* you to bake cookies or change diapers."

God forbid.

"I know, Mother. Yes, I'm sure Jake will understand that a pregnant woman is bound to gain weight and be unsightly."

Apparently talking to her mother on the telephone

was no more pleasant than talking to her in person. But he didn't want to feel sorry for Casey now. No, right now, he wanted to ride the growing wave of anger and disappointment threatening to choke off his air. He wanted to surround himself with it and tell himself that he had been right to be wary. That he had *known* nothing would come of this marriage.

Hurrying through the kitchen, he glanced into the great room, absently noted the still-bare Christmas tree in front of the tall windows, then went on down the hall. He knew where the packages would be. The master bedroom. Where else?

Whenever the UPS man had delivered Linda's never-ending chain of parcels, they'd been piled on the bed so his devoted wife could amuse herself in comfort. Well, he wasn't going to stand by and let it happen all over again. Linda had damn near ruined him with her wild spending and extravagant indulgences. She'd been the only woman he'd ever known who'd actually seemed to *require* a dozen new pairs of shoes every six weeks.

He rounded the corner and spied them immediately—a relatively small stack of packages piled on a chair near the door. Snatching the top one, he ripped off the brown paper, pulled back the lid and stared down at the result of Casey's first foray into spending.

A flannel shirt.

For *him*.

Frowning, Jake quickly went through the rest of the packages, ripping the paper free and tossing it onto the floor. Flannel shirts. Socks. Two pairs of jeans and a rain slicker.

All for him.

Not only that, they were exactly what he would have bought for himself if he'd ever had the time or inclination to shop.

He dropped the last package and shoved one hand through his hair. Confused, he tried to figure out what this might mean. What it did to his theories.

"Well," Casey said dryly from behind him, "I can hardly wait to watch you on Christmas morning."

He turned around to look at her.

She smiled and shook her head at the mess littering the floor. "It's a good thing I didn't have your Christmas present delivered. You're worse than a kid."

"These are all for me," he finally said.

"Is that a problem?" she asked, stepping into the room and picking up a sheet of torn paper from the rug.

"No," he said. Not a problem. *Mystery* was a better word. "But why? When did you get these?"

"At Annie's shop. She had a great catalog there." Both eyebrows lifted. "Don't tell her, but I swiped it.

I didn't think you'd mind, Jake. Your jeans are disintegrating. You stay more wet than dry in your ratty old rain slicker, and I'm afraid Stumbles has developed a taste for your socks."

She'd noticed. She'd shopped for him. Scowling slightly, he bent to pick up the rest of the paper he had tossed about in his frenzy. When he straightened, she looked at him closely.

"My buying clothes for you really surprised you, didn't it?"

"Yeah." He snorted. "You could say that."

"Jeez, Jake, I'm your wife." She shrugged and reached up to plant a quick kiss on his cheek. "I—" Clamping her lips together tightly, she shook her head.

She'd almost said it.

Strange that words *not* said could hurt so much.

"I'm glad you're back," she said in an obvious change of subject. "I'd like to decorate the tree tonight."

"Uh-huh," he answered absently, his brain still adjusting to a woman shopping for him, not herself.

"I was wondering," she went on, speaking a little more loudly to get his attention. "The lights have to go on first. Do you want to do it or would you rather I did?"

"Lights?" he repeated, an image of the tall pine coming to mind. "I'll do it. You'd have to use a ladder, and you might fall."

She nodded. "All right, thanks. Oh, I found an old box of Christmas ornaments in the garage today, so I brought them inside. Hope that's okay."

Now he was really confused. "But I showed you where all the new stuff was yesterday." Every imported glass ball and color-coordinated decoration had cost him a bundle. Naturally Linda hadn't settled for anything but the best.

"Yeah," Casey said slowly, "but it was all so...I don't know. Anyway, I decided to look around for the things I remembered your mother setting out each year."

"Why?" he had to ask.

"OK, Jake," she said, sighing. "The things you showed me yesterday are pretty...but they remind me too much of the professionally decorated trees my mother gets done every year." She shrugged. "For our first Christmas I wanted everything to be..."

"Perfect?"

"Homey," she corrected. "You don't mind if I use your mother's things, do you?"

"No," he said quickly. Of course he didn't mind. He just wasn't sure he understood.

"Good." Casey smiled and turned for the door. "Wash up for dinner, then we'll get this Christmas on the road!"

Christmas, he thought as he sat down on the

mattress. Christmas with his mother's decorations, a real tree and Casey.

He should be happy.

Dammit, why wouldn't he let himself be happy?

Eleven

The next morning bright and early Casey stood in the great room saying goodbye to Jake.

"You'll stay off the ladder?" he asked pointedly.

She chuckled and held up her right hand. "Promise. Besides, I don't need the ladder now." She glanced up at the newly placed strings of lights encircling the floor-to-ceiling front windows. Cheerful Christmas colors shone in the gleaming windowpanes. "Pretty, aren't they?"

"Beautiful," he said softly.

Casey turned to find him staring—not at the lights he'd insisted on hanging himself—but at her. A slow tide of pleasure washed through her. He loved her. She could see it in his eyes whenever he looked at her. Why couldn't he see it, too? Why couldn't he admit to the truth?

"You sure you want to take your car to town?" he asked abruptly. "I could leave the Jeep with you. One of your brothers can drive to the lake."

Casey shook her head. What was this husband of hers going to be like when her pregnancy was further along? He worried about everything, watched her diet like a hawk and *still* couldn't see that he loved her. "You go ahead," she said. "Since you put the snow tires on my car, it's fine. And so am I."

He nodded and grabbed his fishing pole. "I'll be back before dark."

"I'll be here."

He looked at her for a long moment, then bent down to kiss her. What he'd meant to be a brief dusting of lips, Casey instinctively deepened, drawing him closer by looping her arms around his neck.

A low groan eased from the back of his throat, and he dropped the fishing pole to squeeze her tightly. No matter what else lay between them, they shared an incredible magic every time they touched. When she was sure she had his complete attention, she broke the kiss and took a step back. Judging by the tortured expression on his face, her work was done. She might have pretended to go along with his ridiculous notions of what their marriage should be like. But she had never promised to make it easy for him.

"Have fun," she said. "Say hi to Nathan and J.T."

Jake inhaled sharply, narrowed his gaze and jerked her a nod. "I don't have to go fishing, you know."

Though it felt wonderful just knowing he'd be willing to give up a fishing trip with her brothers in favor of being with her, Casey shooed him out of the kitchen. "Yes, you do. The three of you have been talking about going ice fishing since the wedding."

Resigned, he picked up his pole and tackle box and headed for the door. "It seemed like a good idea at the time," he conceded.

"How carving a hole in the ice and sitting all day huddled beside it waiting for a fish to swim by can seem like a good idea at *any* time is beyond me." She smiled, then reached up to tug the collar of his coat higher around his neck.

"You're a girl," he said, wiggling his eyebrows. "Girls don't understand guy stuff."

Maybe not, she thought. But girls understand enough to take advantage when their men were off doing guy stuff. While Jake was busy with her brothers, Casey planned to talk to Annie. She had finally come to the conclusion that, to fight Jake's memories of his ex-wife, she had to know what exactly she was up against.

Dawn was just beginning to creep across the sky, dragging soft rose-colored clouds into the growing brightness. It would be at least another couple of hours before she could call Annie.

She stood at the front window waving until Jake drove out of the yard, then she headed for the warmth of the fireplace. Sitting down with a cup of hot cocoa, she stared into the flames and made her plans.

"She spent nearly every dime the man ever made," Annie said, and reached for another fresh-baked cinnamon roll. "These are really good, Case. But you didn't have to bribe me to make me talk, you know."

"Don't think of it as a bribe. Think of it as an incentive."

Annie arched one black eyebrow and inclined her head. "That *is* easier on my gentle sensibilities."

Incentive, bribe, but what the cinnamon rolls really were, were the products of restless hands and a too-busy brain. Those two hours between dawn and the more respectable 8 a.m. took an alarmingly long time to pass.

"So," Casey said, and reached for Annie's coffeepot, "the reason Jake divorced Linda was that she spent all his money?" that would certainly explain his behavior the day the UPS man made a delivery at the ranch.

"That was part of it, sure. But that wasn't what finally ended it."

Casey glanced over her shoulder toward the living room. She certainly didn't want Lisa wandering in to overhear her mother and aunt discussing her uncle. The muted sounds of an early-morning children's television show drifted to her, along with Lisa's occasional giggle. Stumbles and the little girl had formed an immediate kinship, probably because Lisa believed in sharing her cinnamon roll with the ever-hungry dog.

Turning back to her friend, Casey poured her some more coffee, inhaling the scent wistfully and said, "Tell me."

"First you have to understand, Jake really thought he loved the woman."

Silly that those words could sting. Of course he'd believed he was in love. He'd married the woman, after all. Casey smiled to herself. That didn't prove a thing. He'd married her, too. And seemed determined to prove that he *didn't* love her.

"Frankly," Annie went on, licking icing from her fingertip, "I never did understand what he saw in the woman. She had mean eyes."

Casey grinned and patted her friend's arm. "Thanks. Now, what happened?"

"Simple enough." Annie picked up her coffee cup with both hands. Squeezing the Star Trek memorial mug tightly, she muttered, "He came home early one afternoon and found dear Linda in bed with a BMW salesman from Reno."

"What?"

"Yep." Annie's lips thinned angrily at the memory. "He stood outside his own bedroom door and listened to his wife tell her lover that he shouldn't be worried about her husband finding out. She said Jake was such an idiot for love. He'd forgive her anything."

Good Lord. Emotions raced through Casey, each of them demanding to be recognized. Anger, primarily. At Linda for hurting Jake so. But sympathy for Jake, who'd been so deeply wounded, quickly took precedence.

No wonder he didn't want to talk about love. No wonder he couldn't bring himself to care openly for her. He'd tried it once and had his heart handed back to him in pieces.

"Yeah, it was really ugly for a while," Annie said, and Casey's gaze shot up to meet hers. "But you know, I finally figured out that he couldn't really have loved that bitch."

"What do you mean?"

"He was more furious than hurt. Oh, no doubt, he considers himself lanced to the core." Annie nodded. "Most men tend to attribute gallons more blood than necessary to any wound, no matter how slight."

"Slight?" Casey felt as though she should leap up and defend her husband's right to bleed.

"I'm not saying he wasn't hurt," Annie went on. "Only that it was more like he was embarrassed. For letting himself be such a fool for the wrong woman."

Propping one elbow on the table and cupping her hand in her chin, Casey muttered thoughtfully, "So now he won't be a fool for *any* woman."

"Hey, he'll come around." Annie shrugged. "Eventually."

"I'm not so sure." Casey straightened, reached for a second cinnamon roll and broke it apart before laying it down on her plate. "And why should he?"

"Huh?"

"Well, look at it from his side. He's got a wife. A baby on the way. He knows I love him, but doesn't want to hear about it. He's determined we will have a nice civilized marriage without any of the bother of love."

"Ooh." Annie shuddered. "Sounds cozy."

"Yeah, and I've been going along with it."

"Are you nuts?"

"Mommy," Lisa called from the living room, "I hafta go potty again."

"You go on then, honey. I'll be there in a minute."

"No, I'm not nuts," Casey said, and took a bite of the pastry. She chewed quickly, swallowed and said, "Not anymore, anyway. Dammit, Annie, I've *seen* a civilized marriage. Up close and personal."

Her friend winced in sympathy, and Casey looked away. She knew Annie understood. She'd visited often enough during their growing-up years to see the cool tension between Henderson and Hilary Oakes. Casey's parents had had a so-called successful marriage based on wealth, a love of travel and a closed eye to indiscretions.

But she, Casey, had always dreamed of more. Those dreams had comforted her through long lonely nights and fed her fantasies for years. Most of those fantasies, at least since the time she was fifteen, she admitted silently, had revolved around Jake.

Now she had the chance to make her dreams come true. All she had to do was somehow convince Jake that she really did love him. And that it was safe for him to love her.

"Mommy." Lisa's voice sounded muffled, faraway. "I'm done."

Casey grinned. How did a child manage to put three syllables into a word like "done"?

Annie sighed and stood up. "Get used to the sound of that," she said with a short laugh. "It'll be your turn soon enough."

Alone at the table, Casey sat back in her chair and glanced at the local newspaper. The front-page headline of the *Simpson Salutation* read: HARRY BIGGS WINS CHURCH RAFFLE. And in smaller type, just beneath it: WIFE STUNNED.

She chuckled and picked up the newspaper to read about Harry Biggs's prize. Apparently just about anything could make headlines in a small-town daily.

A smile eased up Casey's features as she stared blankly at the pages in her hand.

She had an idea.

Three days later what she hoped would be the answer to her marital problems lay unopened on the kitchen table. She glanced at the neatly folded newspaper and smiled. It would work, she told herself.

It had to work.

Turning her mind back to the business at hand, she looked down at the pan on the stove and started stirring the contents. Boiling frantically, the mixture of lemon juice and granulated sugar frothed up the sides of the pan. She whisked the bubbles into submission again and again, then scowled when someone knocked on the front door.

Glancing at Stumbles, her fearless protector, Casey laughed. The dog, sound asleep under the kitchen table, hadn't even flinched at the sound.

She glanced down at the filling for her lemon-meringue pie and grimaced. If she took it off the fire now, it would be ruined. If she left it to go answer the door, it would boil over and the kitchen would be a sea of lemony sugar.

Hoping against hope a serial killer wouldn't be so polite as to knock on the door, she hollered, "Come in!"

Keeping the whisk moving rapidly through the frothy mixture, she locked her gaze on the entryway, waiting.

"Casey?"

A deep voice. One she hadn't heard in quite a while. One she'd expected to hear say, "I do," not so very long ago.

Steven.

"Casey?" he called again. "Where are you?"

She cleared her throat, swallowed, then said, "In here."

He stepped into her line of vision through the kitchen doorway and stopped. His gaze shot to hers, and for a long moment, neither of them spoke. Finally he broke the silence.

"Can I come in?"

"You're in already." Taking a deep breath, she told herself there was no point in being nasty. Besides, if she was honest about the whole thing, she was grateful he'd jilted her. If he hadn't taken off for Mexico, she might not have found her way back to Jake. In that spirit she smiled and nodded. "Come on in, Steven."

He seemed to relax then and crossed the main room tugging a muffler from his neck and opening his overcoat as he moved to join her in the kitchen. He looked good. Tanned from his escape to Mexico, his skin was the color of polished brass. Neither as big nor as handsome as Jake, Steven Miller still managed to make female hearts flutter.

Soft brown hair waved back from a high forehead, and his dark brown eyes watched her warily. Dressed in a black overcoat, steel gray suit with a white shirt and a boldly striped red power tie, he looked completely out of place in the homey kitchen, and just as uneasy.

"Oh, relax," she said. She couldn't stand to see him waiting for a blow that wasn't coming. "I'm not going to hit you."

"Not that I'd blame you any," he said with a wry grin. "But I appreciate your restraint."

"What are you doing here, Steven?" And why today? The day she wanted to gather her thoughts for a confrontation with Jake.

"When I got back from Mexico, my mother told me where to find you."

"That's *how* you got here. Not why."

"Right." He ducked his head, peeked into the pan she was still stirring, then straightened and paced the length of the room. He stopped by the fogged-over kitchen windows. When there was a good ten feet separating them, he went on, "I guess I just had to see for myself that you were all right."

"I am now," she said. "I wasn't when I got your note."

He winced and stooped to pet Stumbles, the traitor, who was busy slobbering all over Steven's snow-dusted Gucci loafers. "I *am* sorry about that, Casey."

"That's something, I suppose." She whipped the lemony foam a little more quickly, surprised there was still a small corner of her that was angry at him for what he'd done.

"Look, I tried to talk to you the night before the wedding."

"What?"

"I called your parents' house. Talked to your father." He straightened again, frowning at the slobber on his tassles. "I told him I had to talk to you, but he kept insisting you were not to be disturbed."

Her father? But he hadn't told *her* Steven had called.

"He didn't tell you, did he?"

"That you called? No." She shook her head, denying the cold unsettling feeling creeping into her chest. For some reason, she knew she wasn't going to like whatever else it was he'd come to say.

"Not just that," Steven said softly. "He didn't tell you I wouldn't be at the church."

Her world rocked a bit. Her fingers tightened on the handle of the pan. The knot in her chest tightened until it threatened to choke off her air. Her own father had known her groom wasn't going to put in an appearance at the church. Why hadn't he said anything? Why had he allowed her to go through with it? To be humiliated in front of hundreds of people. She wanted to ask all those questions aloud. She wanted to demand answers to everything. But all she could manage was, "He *knew?*"

"Yeah, he knew. I told him I couldn't go through with it." Steven pushed one hand through his hair, and Casey absently noted that it fell right back into place. "I also told him I didn't think *you* wanted to get married, either." He glanced around the kitchen and smiled sheepishly. "At least, not to me."

"I didn't," she said, and was surprised that her voice worked.

Steven rushed on, barely nodding to acknowledge her statement. "You know your father. He just brushed it all off. Said it was last-minute jitters and I should just show up on time and the marriage would take care of itself." Steven glanced at her and she saw real regret and shame on his features. "I really thought he would tell you, Casey. I never expected you to be there at the church. Waiting."

It sounded like her father, all right. Of course he wouldn't have believed Steven. He never would have believed that someone from their social circle would ruin a carefully arranged and planned wedding. How like Henderson Oakes not to even mention to his daughter the possibility of being jilted.

She felt color rise in her cheeks. "But you were there. You left a note for me."

"Yeah. I drove past the church and saw all the cars. Then I knew that he hadn't said anything." Her ex-fiancé took a few steps closer and stopped. "So I pulled into the parking lot long enough to slip a note to one of my ushers."

"You couldn't come and see me personally?"

"I should have."

"Yeah," she agreed, and turned the fire off. Carrying the pan to the counter where the pie crust was ready and waiting, she poured the mixture in and said, "But I almost understand why you didn't." She got cold chills just thinking about how her parents and his would have reacted to an in-person announcement.

It had been bad enough watching the Oakeses and Millers glaring at each other, each couple blaming the other for the disaster that was their children. If Steven had actually been there, the shouting and the humiliation would have been twice as difficult to bear.

"So," he said, glancing around the house, "are you happy? Mom told me you got married."

"And pregnant."

Two light brown eyebrows lifted.

"I'm *very* happy, Steven," she said. "Actually I ought to thank you. I won't," she added, "but I should."

"I'm glad, Casey." He laughed to fill an awkward silence. "Relieved, too."

She walked up to him and gave him a hug. "You're forgiven, Steven. Relax."

He nodded, then locking his arms around her waist, lifted her off the floor and squeezed her gently. "He's a lucky guy," he said with a chuckle.

Steven's laughter choked off when the back door flew open and crashed against the kitchen wall.

"Damn right," Jake said.

Twelve

Casey's feet hit the floor jarringly enough to rattle her teeth. She looked up at Jake and realized she'd never seen him so angry. Splotches of red, caused not entirely by the cold, stained his cheeks, and his eyes flashed as he looked from Steven to her and back again.

"Goddammit, get your hands off my wife!" Blind with pain, Jake felt like throwing his head back and howling with the rage boiling through him.

"It's not what you think," the man said.

"Calm down, Jake." Casey faced him, meeting his gaze squarely. "You're acting like a nut." Hurriedly she closed the kitchen door to shut out the frigid air.

She was criticizing *his* behavior?

The other man spoke again. "Look. Maybe I'd better just introduce myself and we can start over." He extended his right hand. "My name's Steven Miller."

Steven.

Jake shot a look at Casey and read her expression easily enough. Glancing back at the expensively dressed man, he gave himself over to the pulse-pounding anger throbbing within. He had never before really known what it meant when people said they were so angry they "saw red." Until now. It wasn't bad enough that he had *again* walked into his own house and found his wife in the arms of another man. No, this time, it had to be *the* other man. The man she had intended to marry.

Pain, white-hot and insistent, shimmered inside him. Before he knew what he was doing, he took a single step forward, batted the man's hand out of his way and slammed his fist into his jaw.

Jake felt the satisfying thud all the way up his arm. He watched with grim vindication as the intruder staggered backward into the table. The man's fall knocked an unfinished lemon pie to the floor, crust and filling splashed across the tiles. Stumbles shot out from under the table and rushed for the fallen goodies. The man wobbled unsteadily and dropped to the floor, one hand clapped to his jaw.

It was only then that Jake turned to look at his wife again. His heart hammered in his chest. His brain raced. His blood was still boiling. Despite his fears, he'd never really expected Casey to cheat on him. Nor had he expected the depth of pain betrayal would bring.

What he had lived through at Linda's hands seemed insignificant in comparison. This pain stabbed at him. Slashed at him. Every moment that passed only made the ache worse.

"Are you out of your mind?" Casey shouted.

"What?" His breathing labored, he stared at her. What did *she* have to be angry about?

Bending down, she helped the other man to his feet. It didn't make Jake feel any better to notice that the guy carefully kept his distance from Casey once he was standing.

"Why did you hit him?" she demanded.

"Why was he holding *my* wife?"

"It was a hug, Jake. Just a hug." She waved one hand at the mess on the floor being slurped up by a happy dog. "I was baking a pie, Jake. This is the kitchen, for God's sake. Not the bedroom."

He lifted one black eyebrow, silently demanding that she remember the time he and she had used the kitchen as a trysting place.

She flushed, and he knew the memory had come to her.

"I know what I saw, Casey." Why couldn't she understand what it had felt like to see her in someone else's arms?

"You saw what you've been expecting to see." She lifted her chin and looked him dead in the eye. "You've been waiting for something like this since the day we got married."

"What?" Had she known all along what was going through his mind?

"You didn't think I knew, did you?"

He sighed. "Annie."

"Yes, Annie. Your *sister* told me everything that *you* should have told me."

His chest tightened. He hadn't wanted her to know. Hadn't wanted Casey to know that his ex-wife had thought so little of him that she had flaunted her lovers in his own house. Jesus, what kind of thing was that for a man to know about himself? Did she really think he would want to tell *her?*

"There was no reason for you to know about Linda. It had nothing to do with us." He folded his arms across his chest in an unconscious but useless attempt to hold his heart in place.

"Nothing to do with us?" Casey moved forward then stopped again.

"Excuse me," Steven said from his position behind her. "Perhaps I should be leaving."

"Shut up," Jake said.

"Shut up," Casey snapped at the same time.

Steven shrugged and turned to watch the gorging dog.

"How can you say what happened with Linda has nothing to do with us?" Casey demanded.

"It happened a long time ago," Jake said.

"And what happened then has colored everything that has passed between us."

"Casey—"

"No, let's get it said. Finally let's get it said."

Jake flinched away from the sheen of tears he saw sparkling in her eyes. His entire body ached with the urge to run from the room. To put the pain aside. To forget seeing Casey in Steven's arms and just go back to the way things had been between them.

In a last-ditch attempt to postpone the inevitable, he said as much. "Stop, Casey. Stop now. We can forget all about what happened today."

Steven snorted.

They ignored him.

"We can go back to the way we were," Jake went on. "It was all right, wasn't it?"

"'All right' isn't good enough, Jake," she said quietly. "Not anymore. I want to be loved. I want a *real* marriage. And in real marriages, people talk to each other. Trust each other." Her bottom lip quivered a bit, but she charged ahead. "For weeks you've been watching, waiting for me to do something that would prove to you I was just like Linda. You've been holding your breath, almost hoping for the chance to say, 'See? I knew I shouldn't love you.' Instead of realizing I am *nothing* like Linda, instead of snatching at our chance for happiness, you chose to sit back and throw stones at everything we had."

"I never said you were like Linda."

She sucked in a breath and let her gaze slide over him slowly before looking into his eyes again. Disappointment filled her, and Casey shook her head slowly. "You didn't have to say it. It was there. Between us. Every day." She snatched her purse from the counter, then reached back and grabbed hold of Steven's jacket. Tugging her ex-fiancé toward the door, she told her husband, "Fine, then, Jake. If you think what you saw is enough reason to throw away my love, great. You win. Now you don't have to put up with me."

"Where are you going?" Jake moved closer.

"Why do you care?" She shoved Steven through the open door, grabbed her coat and glared at the man she loved. "I don't understand how I could be so in love with a man as impossibly arrogant and stupid and pigheaded as you, Jake Parrish!" Walking into the mudroom, she snapped, "But if I try *really* hard, maybe I'll get over it."

Then she was gone and his only company was a delighted dog and the echo of the door slamming shut.

"Where are we?"

Casey blinked and looked at Steven. "What did you say?"

He worked his jaw back and forth, then said again, "Where are we?"

She glanced at the building directly in front of them. Holiday paintings decorated the windows of Annie's beauty shop. She almost sneered at Santa and his happy elves. Strange, she didn't even remember heading for Annie's place. But then, she hardly remembered the drive into town, either. So angry at Jake she could hardly speak, she had simply demanded Steven's keys, climbed into the driver's seat of his Porsche and taken off with Steven in the passenger seat.

Vaguely she recalled hearing her ex-fiancé groan when she occasionally failed to engage the clutch of his precious car, but she'd ignored him. Every ounce of her being was too filled with images of her husband for her to think of anything else.

Of all the hardheaded, insulting, chest-pounding Neanderthals she'd ever known, Jake Parrish took the prize.

Imagine that fool actually believing that she would cheat on him! Oh, she understood about Linda. Fine, the woman had been a treacherous bitch. But for him to tar her with the same brush was unforgivable.

"Casey," Steven said, "do you know a good doctor in town? I really think I ought to have my jaw looked at."

She glared at him briefly. "You're talking, Steven. It's not broken."

"I don't know." He held one hand to his cheek and worked his jaw again. "I hear it popping when I do this."

"Then don't do that." Grumbling under her breath, Casey opened the car door and got out, slamming the door behind her.

She didn't wait for him to follow her. Instead, she stomped through the few feet of slush to the beauty parlor and went inside.

The silence was deafening.

Jake rolled his shoulders, glanced at the dog and scowled. "What are *you* smiling about?"

Stumbles ducked his head and scuttled out of the room.

Disgusted with himself and the whole situation, Jake started pacing, his boots clicking angrily against the tiles.

"What did she expect me to think?" he demanded of no one. "I come in the door to my own house and find her with another man and I'm not supposed to be mad?"

His words echoed back at him and he flinched at the loneliness of the sound. He came to a sudden stop and looked down at the now shiny-clean pie plate. Stumbles had eaten every last crumb.

Lemon meringue.

Jake's favorite.

She'd been making his favorite pie. From scratch. For him.

His gaze shifted to the table where the day's paper lay alongside an opened Christmas catalog and a list of gifts to buy for Lisa, Annie, his aunt and uncle, and his father.

Casey had been thinking about him. She was always thinking about him.

"Then *I* walk in the door and start acting like some deranged actor in a third-rate play." He slumped against the cooking island and let his mind drift back over the past several weeks.

Laughter had filled the house. There was a warmth

to the place that hadn't been there since he was a child. Even now the scent of the Christmas tree wafted to him, making him feel the season as he hadn't in a very long time. Every time he walked through the door, he felt the welcome in the air. Felt Casey's love.

For weeks he'd been surrounded by that love. Somehow he'd been given a second chance at happiness. That too-young girl he'd wanted so badly five years before had come back into his life and given him everything he'd ever dreamed of.

And he'd allowed his fear of losing that happiness to ensure that he did.

Of course she wasn't like Linda. On some gut level, he'd always known that. It was only his pride that had kept him from acknowledging it until now, when it was too late. Had she left him for good? Was she so disgusted with him she was never coming back? And could he live without her?

No.

He couldn't.

"So, what are you going to do?" he muttered, and braced both hands on the cooking island behind him. His mind filled with images of Casey and chocolate éclairs and long slow deep kisses.

His imagination drew mental pictures of Casey—in a few more months her belly round and heavy with their child. Her warm smile and the gleam in her eyes as she looked at him.

Abruptly he pushed away from the counter and raced outside. There was only one thing he *could* do. Get her back. Where she belonged.

With him.

"Casey!" Annie called out a welcome as the door flew open. "I was going to call you in a few minutes. I just saw the newspaper."

Casey cringed and glanced around the tiny shop, dismayed to find one customer in the chair and two other women on the sofa waiting their turns.

She didn't want to talk about the ad she'd taken out in the local paper. Not now. Not when everything had changed so drastically. Dammit, she'd had such high hopes that the ad in the paper would convince Jake to take a chance on their happiness.

"What's wrong?" Annie asked, and walked toward her friend and sister-in-law, customers forgotten.

"What *isn't* wrong?" Casey muttered. "That would take far less time."

"Oh, no. What did Jake do now?"

The front door opened again and Annie's gaze shifted to the newcomer.

"Annie," Casey said on a sigh. "Meet Steven."

"Steven? *The* Steven?"

"Why did that sound like '*The* Jack the Ripper'?" Steven asked.

"Sorry. Jeez," Annie winced in sympathy "—what happened to you? Your cheek is purple." Her gaze shot to Casey. "Jake?"

"Jake."

"I don't mean to be a bother," Steven interrupted. "But could I have some ice, do you think?"

"Sure. Get it yourself." Annie jerked her head toward the back room.

Steven's eyebrows lifted, but he went.

Annie turned to Casey. "What's going on?"

"Annie, I don't even know. Jake came in the house, found me hugging Steven and slugged him."

"Oh, boy."

Rushed whispers erupted from the corner waiting area, and Casey glanced at the two middle-aged women. Immediately the pair straightened up and pretended an air of casual disinterest. The customer in Annie's chair didn't bother to pretend. She had her neck craned back so far to listen that Casey was surprised her head didn't snap off.

Too bad for Jake, she thought. He hated gossip so much he really shouldn't go around hitting people.

Steven came back into the room just then, a

sandwich bag full of ice held to his jaw. His interested gaze swept over Annie slowly, appreciatively. When he met her steely blue eyes, he shrugged helplessly, then looked at Casey.

"Will you be all right here if I leave?"

"Running out on her again, eh?" Annie said.

He stiffened. "I didn't run out on her."

"Jilt's an ugly word."

The whispering started up in the corner again, and Casey sighed. She was going to be the subject of Simpson gossip for months. If not years. Decades from now, her grandchildren would be hearing the story of the day their grandma's old boyfriend had come to town and how their granddaddy had cleaned his clock.

"Of course she'll be all right," Annie snapped. "Why wouldn't she be?"

"I didn't mean to imply anything."

Casey looked away from them. She didn't have the energy to referee. She stared through the window at Main Street, hardly noticing the brightly colored plastic candy canes that hung from the lampposts or the evergreen swags stretched across the narrow drive. Casey sighed tiredly and felt what little strength she had left disappear as Jake drove up. She frowned when he parked the Jeep directly behind Steven's car, blocking it from moving.

* * *

"Hey, Jake," Mr. Holbrook at the hardware store said. "Congratulations."

Jake smiled, nodded and wondered what the hell the man was talking about.

"I think it's just so sweet!" This from an older female voice. Jake turned to see Dolly Fenwick grinning at him from the sidewalk. "And so romantic," she continued with a heavy sigh. "You tell Casey I said Merry Christmas."

He nodded. What was going on? Jake glanced at the car Casey had sped away in. Blocked by the Jeep, that Porsche wasn't going anywhere. At least not if Casey tried to leave in it.

Hurrying to the beauty shop, he opened the door and stepped into the most important fight of his life.

Steven dropped his ice bag, bent his knees and lifted both fists like an old-fashioned prizefighter. Bobbing and weaving, he prepared for battle.

Jake frowned at him. "I didn't come here for you," he said.

Steven's eyebrows lifted, but he slowly dropped his fists, still keeping a wary eye on Jake.

"Why *did* you come?" Casey asked tiredly.

"I came to get you."

"Why? Afraid I stole the family silver?"

There was a muffled snort from the cluster of chairs in the corner.

"Dammit, Casey!" He realized he was shouting so he lowered his voice. "I came to take you home."

"I'm not going home."

"Atta girl," somebody murmured.

"You're not leaving me." Amazing he was able to squeeze those words out past the tightness in his throat. He glanced around the little shop, from his sister's disgusted expression to Steven and to the older ladies watching him with open interest. He dismissed them all. He didn't care who heard him. He didn't care if people talked about him for weeks. All he knew was that he had to convince his wife to give him another chance. He only hoped he could figure out the right things to say. "I won't let you leave me, Casey."

"Leave *you?*" Surprise tinged her voice.

"Everything you said is true," Jake blurted, and stepped closer to her. "I was a jerk. I was standing back and trying not to care. But I cared, anyway."

"You did?" She cocked her head and watched him carefully.

"Of course I did." He closed the space between them, but didn't touch her. He couldn't risk that yet. If she moved away from him, it would hurt too much. "I loved you from the beginning, Casey."

"Say that again."

He smiled. "I love you. Always have. Please, Casey, don't leave me. Stumbles and I would never survive."

Her lips twitched. "A dirty trick, using Stumbles against me."

"I'm desperate."

"How desperate."

"Enough to try anything. Say anything. Casey, I love you. Come home with me. Give me the chance to prove to you I can be foolishly lovesick as well as anybody." Risking it now, he placed both hands on her shoulders. "Don't leave me, Casey." He lowered his voice and bent his head so only she would hear him say, "If you leave, the loneliness and the pain will kill me."

"You big dummy."

He blinked and jerked his head back. "What?"

"You are such a dummy, Jake." She grinned at him and shook her head. "I wasn't going to leave you."

"You weren't?" The knot in his chest loosened, and breath came easily again to his straining lungs.

"Of course not." She reached up and smoothed one hand over his cheek. He turned his face into her touch. "I don't give up *that* easy," she said solemnly. "You're an aggravating man sometimes, Jake, but I love you."

He pulled in another breath.

"I don't *stop* loving you just because I'm angry. I

only left the house because I needed to get away before I gave you the swift kick you deserved."

"From now on I give you permission to kick me whenever I need it."

"I'll remember that," she told him. Turning her head slightly, she looked at Annie. Her sister-in-law was grinning from ear to ear and wiping away a trickle of tears. "Hand me the newspaper, please."

Confused, Jake watched his sister grab the *Salutation* and slap it into Casey's waiting hand.

"If you read the paper in the morning like everybody else in town," Casey said, "you would have seen this hours ago." Opening up the front page, she held it in front of her like a shield and waited for him to read it.

Jake's gaze swept the headline once, then again, just to assure himself he wasn't imagining things. But he wasn't. A smile spread slowly across his face. Now he understood what the people outside had been talking about. No doubt everyone in town would be discussing it for weeks.

But *this* kind of gossip he could grow to like.

He looked at the headline one last time and felt the last of his doubts and worries slip away. Right across the top of the page in bold black letters were the words: CASEY LOVES JAKE: A FOOL FOR LOVE.

He lifted his gaze to his wife's smiling face. Taking

the newspaper from her, he tossed it to the floor and reached for her. He held her close to him and felt his world come right again.

With Casey in his arms, he had everything he would ever need. Looking down at her, he whispered, "I guess being a fool for love can be a good thing."

She nodded. "If the fool you're in love with loves you right back."

Then he kissed her, long and deep, and neither one of them heard the applause from the delighted onlookers.

Epilogue

Christmas afternoon...

"We really should get busy," Casey said, and snuggled closer. She and Jake were lying on the couch. "You know everyone will be here soon."

"No hurry," her husband muttered, holding her more tightly to his side.

She laughed and lifted her head to look down at him. "You've been saying that all day, Jake."

Of course, she wasn't complaining. Why would she? Spending Christmas day making love to a husband who adored her was a dream come true.

He smiled as he ran one fingertip across her jaw. "A man's entitled to spend his first Christmas with his new wife any way he chooses."

"Is that so?" One eyebrow arched high on her forehead.

He nodded. "It's a rule, I think."

Chuckling softly, she laid her head on his chest and stared at the Christmas tree, its lights blazing, its odd assortment of well-loved ornaments looking somehow…regal.

"It's a perfect Christmas, isn't it?" she whispered.

"Perfect," he repeated, and wrapped both arms around her. Outside, snow twisted in a cold wind and slapped against the windows. But inside, a fire burned, both in the hearth and between the two people lying so close on the sofa.

Beneath the Christmas tree a small mound of presents, wrapped in festive paper, lay waiting to be opened and appreciated. Close by, Stumbles snored gently, lost in dreams.

"Don't you want to open your present before your family gets here?" Casey asked as she listened to the steady beat of his heart beneath her ear.

"Nope," he said, stroking her back gently. "I've already got my presents."

She tipped her head back to look up at him and

found him watching her through eyes that no longer hid his love. "You do?"

"I do. The only present I'll ever need is you. And the baby. And you."

She smiled. "You already said that."

"I want to say it. Over and over. As many times as you can stand to hear it." Cupping her cheek with one hand, he said, "I love you, Casey. More than I ever thought possible. Every day with you is magic. Every day is Christmas."

Tears stung her eyes, but she blinked them back before raising herself high enough to kiss him gently. "I love you, too, Jake. Merry Christmas."

"Merry Christmas."

Then he kissed her, and when she closed her eyes, she could still see brightly colored lights twinkling merrily.

* * * * *

SPECIAL EDITION

Life, Love and Family

*These contemporary romances will strike a chord
with you as heroines juggle life
and relationships on their way to true love.*

New York Times *bestselling author Linda Lael
Miller brings you a BRAND-NEW contemporary
story featuring her fan-favorite McKettrick family.*

Meg McKettrick is surprised to be reunited with
her high school flame, Brad O'Ballivan. After
enjoying a career as a country-and-western singer,
Brad aches for a home and family…and seeing
Meg again makes him realize he still loves her. But
their pride manages to interfere with love…until
an unexpected matchmaker gets involved.

*Turn the page for a sneak preview of
THE McKETTRICK WAY
by Linda Lael Miller
On sale November 20, wherever books are sold.*

Brad shoved the truck into gear and drove to the bottom of the hill, where the road forked. Turn left, and he'd be home in five minutes. Turn right, and he was headed for Indian Rock.

He had no damn business going to Indian Rock.

He had nothing to say to Meg McKettrick, and if he never set eyes on the woman again, it would be two weeks too soon.

He turned right.

He couldn't have said why.

He just drove straight to the Dixie Dog Drive-In.

Back in the day, he and Meg used to meet at the Dixie Dog, by tacit agreement, when either of them had been away. It had been some kind of universe thing, purely intuitive.

Passing familiar landmarks, Brad told himself he ought to turn around. The old days were gone. Things had ended badly between him and Meg anyhow, and she wasn't going to be at the Dixie Dog.

He kept driving.

He rounded a bend, and there was the Dixie Dog. Its big neon sign, a giant hot dog, was all lit up and going through its corny sequence—first it was covered in red squiggles of light, meant to suggest ketchup, and then yellow, for mustard.

Brad pulled into one of the slots next to a speaker, rolled down the truck window and ordered.

A girl roller-skated out with the order about five minutes later.

When she wheeled up to the driver's window, smiling, her eyes went wide with recognition, and she dropped the tray with a clatter.

Silently Brad swore. Damn if he hadn't forgotten he was a famous country singer.

The girl, a skinny thing wearing too much eye makeup, immediately started to cry. "I'm sorry!" she sobbed, squatting to gather up the mess.

"It's okay," Brad answered quietly, leaning to look down at her, catching a glimpse of her plastic name tag. "It's okay, Mandy. No harm done."

"I'll get you another dog and a shake right away, Mr. O'Ballivan!"

"Mandy?"

She stared up at him pitifully, sniffling. Thanks to the copious tears, most of the goop on her eyes had slid south. "Yes?"

"When you go back inside, could you not mention seeing me?"

"But you're Brad O'Ballivan!"

"Yeah," he answered, suppressing a sigh. "I know."

She rolled a little closer. "You wouldn't happen to have a picture you could autograph for me, would you?"

"Not with me," Brad answered.

"You could sign this napkin, though," Mandy said. "It's only got a little chocolate on the corner."

Brad took the paper napkin and her order pen, and scrawled his name. Handed both items back through the window.

She turned and whizzed back toward the side entrance to the Dixie Dog.

Brad waited, marveling that he hadn't considered incidents like this one before he'd decided to come back home. In retrospect, it seemed shortsighted, to say the least, but the truth was, he'd expected to be—Brad O'Ballivan.

Presently Mandy skated back out again, and this time she managed to hold on to the tray.

"I didn't tell a soul!" she whispered. "But Heather and Darlene *both* asked me why my mascara was all smeared." Efficiently she hooked the tray onto the bottom edge of the window.

Brad extended payment, but Mandy shook her head.

"The boss said it's on the house, since I dumped your first order on the ground."

He smiled. "Okay, then. Thanks."

Mandy retreated, and Brad was just reaching for the food when a bright red Blazer whipped into the space beside his. The driver's door sprang open, crashing into the metal speaker, and somebody got out in a hurry.

Something quickened inside Brad.

And in the next moment Meg McKettrick was standing practically on his running board, her blue eyes blazing.

Brad grinned. "I guess you're not over me after all," he said.

Silhouette

SPECIAL EDITION™

**brings you a heartwarming
new McKettrick's story from**

NEW YORK TIMES BESTSELLING AUTHOR

LINDA LAEL MILLER

THE McKETTRICK *Way*

Meg McKettrick is surprised to be reunited with her high school flame, Brad O'Ballivan, who has returned home to his family's neighboring ranch. After seeing Meg again, Brad realizes he still loves her. But the pride of both manage to interfere with love...until an unexpected matchmaker gets involved.

—— McKettrick Women ——

Available December wherever you buy books.

Visit Silhouette Books at www.eHarlequin.com SSEIBC24867

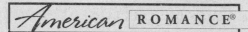

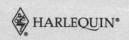

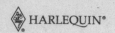

EVERLASTING LOVE™

Every great love has a story to tell™

Every Christmas gift Will and Dinah
exchange is a symbol of their love.
The tradition began on their very first
date and continues through every holiday
season—whether they're together or apart—
until tragedy strikes. And then only an
unexpected gift can make things right.

Look for

*Christmas Presents
and Past*

by
Janice Kay Johnson

Available December wherever you buy books.